Gruff Love

A Reverse Harem Fairy Tale Retelling

USA Today Bestselling Author

Cassidy K. O'Connor

Gruff Love © 2021 Cassidy K. O'Connor

Cover design by B Creative Design
Formatting by Celtic Formatting

Dedication

To my sister Sheri Lyn, I hope I did justice to your favorite fairy tale.

Chapter One

The storm raging outside the small farmhouse was nothing compared to the one going on inside the home. The Gruff brothers sat at the kitchen table and argued in hushed whispers. They didn't want their parents to hear their discussion and make themselves sicker than they already were.

Jakob, the eldest brother, slapped his hand on his thigh. "We have to think of something and soon. We're almost out of food and the crops didn't yield enough to be worth much at the market."

Henrik, the middle brother held his head in his hands, his thumbs rubbing circles on his temples. "We've sold off everything of value. I checked with some of the neighboring farms, everyone is in the same situation."

The youngest brother, Filip, jumped to his feet and paced the kitchen. "This is all the King's fault. Ever since the Queen and Princess died, he's let the Kingdom go to ruin. I heard he has parties almost every night. How is that gluttonous pig able to hold lavish events while his people starve to death?"

Jakob held his hands up to shush his little brother. "You can't speak that way of your King. You'll be thrown in the dungeon for treason."

Henrik rolled his eyes. "It's torrentially pouring outside; who can possibly hear us?"

Jakob shrugged. "You know as well as I do that he speaks his mind too freely. He needs to learn to be more careful regardless of where he is. I'm in charge of this family now and I won't let anything happen to either of you."

Filip plopped back into his chair and let out a dejected sigh. "I'm sorry; I'm not trying to make things harder on you. I actually called you both in here to tell you I'm leaving."

The other two brothers sat forward and Filip held his hand up to stop them from interrupting. "I heard of a Blacksmith over in Pruthage who is hiring. I'm going to see if he'll hire me. I'll send a letter letting you both know if I got the job. I'll come home every other weekend with any money I've earned. Who knows, maybe he'll be able to hire one of you as well."

Jakob crossed his arms across his chest, his eyebrows were drawn together. "That's a three-day ride and there's still plenty of work to be done here."

Filip shook his head. "It's just over two day's ride if I take the Cressian Bridge."

Jakob slammed his fist on the table. "Absolutely not. We've all heard the rumors that there is something in that part of the forest hunting people.

Take the long way around."

Filip knew better than to argue with his brother. "Fine, it will take me twice as long but if that's what I have to do to get you to agree to let me go, I'll do it."

Henrik cleared his throat. "And what if Mother or Father passes while you are gone? You'll never forgive yourself."

Filip swallowed loudly. Nerves made his voice shake. "That won't happen; you'll keep them well and it's only long enough for me to learn what I need to so I can come back here and start my own business."

Jakob sighed heavily. "I don't like it but I agree we've run out of options. Send a message as soon as you've arrived letting us know if you are staying or returning."

Filip's shoulders sagged with relief. He expected his brothers to put up a bigger fight. Just because Jakob was the oldest at twenty-three, and Henrik at Twenty, they felt the need to protect Filip. He was eighteen now and wanted to help save his parents. The lack of food had really taken a toll on his parent's health and he wasn't going to stand by and watch them waste away.

He ran to his room and packed quickly, only grabbing enough clothes to fill one satchel. He glanced around his room one final time before going to visit his parents. He knocked gently on their door as he entered. His parents laid in bed sleeping quietly. He leaned down and kissed his mother's cheek.

Her eyes fluttered open. "Filip, why do you look worried?"

He brushed a strand of hair from her face. "I'm going to be gone for a bit. I'm going to try to get work nearby. I wanted to say goodbye before I left."

She reached over and shook her husband awake. He grunted as he rolled over. "What, what is it?"

His mother reached for his hand. "Filip is leaving."

His father, once strong and broad-chested, was now frail and thin. "Why are you leaving? There's plenty of work for you here."

Filip chuckled. It was no surprise he said nearly the identical argument that Jakob had. "We've talked about this; we need more money than the farm is providing. Jakob and Henrik will manage until I return."

His mother squeezed his hand. "I don't like it, you shouldn't go."

Filip leaned down and kissed the top of her head. "I promise to be safe. I'll be back before you know it."

With one last look at his parents, he walked out and made his way to the barn.

His brothers stood next to one of the horses already saddled. Henrik patted a sack tied to the saddle. "I've packed a few meals for you. It should be enough to get you to Pruthage."

Jakob handed him a tiny bag of coins. Filip tried to give it back. "Take the money; you don't know what may happen while you're out there."

Filip shook his head. "How will you buy food this week?"

Jakob crossed his arms over his chest. "We'll manage just fine. I'm more worried about you. I'm going along with this plan of yours so don't push it; take the money."

Filip swallowed past the lump in his throat as he tucked the bag into his jacket pocket. "Take care while I'm gone. I promise to send a letter as soon as I get there."

They had always been a close family but it still felt strange when each of his brothers pulled him close and hugged him tightly. Even though he'd never spent one night away from them, he was excited to be leaving. He knew he was doing what was necessary to save their lives.

He climbed on the horse and with one final wave rode out of the barn. He ignored the ominous feeling in the pit of his stomach. No amount of feelings of impending doom would stop him from trying to help his family. He sent up a silent prayer that this wouldn't be the last time he saw his home.

Chapter Two

Filip rolled his head from one shoulder to the other. He'd been riding for hours only stopping long enough to rest the horse and go to the bathroom. As exhausted as he was of sitting in his saddle, he was also excited to be on his first adventure alone.

All thoughts of being tired disappeared as the Cressian Bridge came into view. He felt a tiny bit of guilt for lying to his brothers but it wasn't enough to make him take an extra two days just to avoid this path.

As he got closer, he noticed the birds stopped chirping. The wind whistled through the trees, almost as if warning him to go back.

A sound off to his right had him whipping his head that way, then movement out of the corner of his eye had him twisting the other way. "Come on, Filip, calm down, you're not a child any longer."

As the horse approached the entrance to the bridge, a foul odor made him gag. It was the smell of death. His hands tightened on the reins with the intention of turning the horse around when a roar sounded behind him just as something hard cracked against his skull.

***

Filip's head felt like it had been split open. The pain was so intense he was afraid to open his eyes and risk light making the ache worse. He slowly reached up and rubbed his scalp; not surprised to find it felt sticky and wet. A picture of Jakob standing over him saying, "I told you not to use the bridge," had Filip groaning out loud.

Something nearby immediately reacted to his moan and started moving around. The person or more likely the creature, given the smell that was wafting from it, grunted and snorted as it walked around the cave.

Filip gathered his courage before opening his eyes, determined to confront the creature and fight for his life.

He took a deep breath, then dared to look around. They were deep in a cave; a fire crackled on the other side of the cavern. He sat up slowly and reached toward the vines hanging in front of him. Panic set in as he realized they weren't hanging from the ceiling, but he was imprisoned within a cage made from ropes. Maybe it wasn't a creature after all; he doubted an animal would know how to make a cage as sophisticated as this was.

The snorting got louder as a large, dark figure came shuffling back into the cave. He watched as it added logs to the fire. Filip had never seen anything like the creature before. It was shaped like a human but was covered in thick, matted hair. Its back was curved and lumps protruded from all over its body.

Filip shuddered just looking at the thing. He didn't know if it was man or beast but either way it wasn't here to be friends.

He quietly stepped to the side of the cage and tested the vines, hoping to find a weak area all the while keeping an eye on the monster. He watched it bend over and pick up something off the ground and stick it over the fire. The smell of cooking meat reached his nose forcing his stomach to growl in hunger. He must have been unconscious longer than he'd realized.

Filip grew angrier by the moment as he realized the cage was built perfectly. He backed against the wall as the creature got up and walked toward him. Filip wanted plenty of room to fight off the beast.

It stuck its hairy arm through a hole in the cage and held something out to him.

Filip growled in frustration when it just stood there staring and saying nothing. "What do you want?"

The creature grunted and waved its hand at him again. He wasn't about to get any closer than he had to. He crossed his arms and stared back at the creature. Finally, it sighed like a human before dropping whatever was in its hand and stomped out of the cave.

Filip scurried over to see what was on the

ground. It was half of the rabbit that had been cooking over the fire. *Why is it feeding me? To fatten me up?*

He ate a few pieces greedily then went back to testing the cage more aggressively while he was alone. "Damn it." He shook the cage hard, until exhausted and out of breath. Filip sat back against the wall while his head pounded and his stomach growled. If he was going to get out of here, he needed strength. He grabbed the rabbit and slowed down to enjoy each bite. It had been a long time since he'd had that much meat in one meal.

He dozed off until noise at the cave entrance jerked him awake. The creature was back with its arms full of something shiny. It crossed to another wall and dropped the objects. It turned and sat by the fire. Filip studied the pile, his heart dropped into his stomach. It was a mound of helmets, shields, and swords from the palace guards. They were covered in blood. His mind raced trying to piece together what was going on. *Where are the soldiers' bodies? If it killed them, why didn't it kill him? Was it hunting soldiers, and, if so, why?*

The creature tossed more wood on the fire then laid down and went to sleep. Filip had no choice but to sleep and gain his strength. He had to escape and get a note to his brothers before they came looking for him. Not that they would find him; if he had listened like a good brother should, he wouldn't be a prisoner right now because he would have avoided Cressian bridge.

A single tear rolled down his cheek. He swiped it away then turned and listened intently to a new sound coming from across the cave. If he didn't know better, he would swear the monster was crying and it sounded decidedly feminine.

Chapter Three

F ilip jumped awake when the monster growled. It stood at the door to his cage holding a piece of wood with meat and fruit on it. It held the plate between the ropes and motioned for him to take it. He took a few steps toward the food and reached for the wood. The monster turned to walk away. "I have to go to the bathroom."

The creature froze for a few seconds, and then walked over to the mound of weapons. It grabbed a rope and walked back over to him. The troll grunted as it held its arms out and put its wrists together. *How is a troll this intelligent?*

Filip held his wrists together and waited while the beast tied the rope. It opened the door to the cage and yanked him out. The troll bent down and tied more of the rope around his feet and then pointed to the cave entrance.

Filip shuffled out and blinked as the sun hit his face. The troll shoved his back to keep him moving. "I'm walking as fast as I can. If I promise not to run will you undo my hands? As soon as I'm done you can tie them back up."

The creature stared at him, he held his hands out and waited. It had to know between its size and strength and his feet tied he had no chance of getting away.

The troll reached up and undid the knot at his wrists and waved at him to keep walking. Then the creature slackened the rope and stayed by the cave entrance to give him privacy.

He rushed through his business and leaned against a tree while taking a deep breath. He had no idea how he was going to get out of here but he had to try soon.

A rough tug of the rope was all he needed to know the troll grew impatient with him.

He shuffled out from behind the tree and held his hands out for the monster to bind him again. The troll stared at his hands while fastening rope around them. "Thank you, I appreciate it."

It glanced up at him, then turned and pulled him into the cave. Instead of dragging him toward the cage it led him to the fire and pointed at the ground.

"You want me to sit?" The troll grunted at Filip's question. "I'll take that as a yes."

An awkward silence filled the cave as they stared into the flames. When Filip couldn't take the quiet any longer, he turned and looked at the troll. "So, are you from around here?" The creature glanced at him out of the side of its eyes but didn't respond. "My family and I have a farm on the other side of the Kingdom, it's a two-day ride from here."

Silence enveloped them once again for a few minutes.

Filip twiddled his thumbs. "So, do you have family around here? Any troll babies running around the forest?"

Filip chuckled at his own joke. The creature must not have appreciated his humor. It jumped up, grabbed him by the arm, and dragged him to the cage. Confused by what set the beast off, he stumbled trying to keep up. He was thrown in the cage and the door was shut tight. It stuck its arms through the holes and grunted at him. Filip held up his hands and let it untie the rope. He bent over and undid the ropes at his feet. As soon as he was free the creature yanked the rope out of the cage, tossed it on the pile of weapons, and stormed out of the cave.

Filip sighed. "Good to know, no talking about family."

Chapter Four

Filip laid on the floor of his cage staring at the barely visible walls. The troll hadn't returned and the fire had died down hours earlier. He tried to ignore the creeping fear of being abandoned and unable to escape.

Noise from the cave entrance had him sitting up. The troll walked by dragging something. He stayed silent and watched as it built the fire back up.

With light filling the cavern again, he could see the large turkey the troll killed. Filip's stomach growled loudly, and he couldn't remember the last time he had eaten one.

The troll grabbed the turkey and plucked feathers from the bird.

Filip was tired of being in the cage and afraid if she stayed mad at him, she wouldn't let him out again. "I don't mind helping pluck the animal if you want?" She stopped what she was doing and stared at him. "You can tie my ankles again, I don't mind."

She watched him for a full minute before getting up, grabbing the rope, and opening the cage. He stood silently as she tied his ankles and led him back to the fire.

Filip shuffled over and sat next to her. She ignored him as she went back to plucking feathers. He reached over and pulled a few out. "This reminds me of a time when I was maybe six or seven years old. My father came home from the market one day with a surprise for everyone. He'd bought a turkey for us. My brother's and I had never eaten one before. Unfortunately, the turkey was still alive. For a few days, it lived on the farm. Henrik, who's two years older than me took a liking to the animal. He treated it more like a pet, spent all his free time with it. My father kept warning him not to get attached but Henrik couldn't help himself. When the time came to slaughter and eat him Henrik cried the entire day. That night at dinner as the bird was served to us we were all miserable as we ate it. Henrik refused to even try it."

Filip laughed to himself at the memory. A weird gurgling noise had him looking up. If he didn't know better, he would say the troll was laughing, either that or choking, but given the story he just told, he opted to believe she was trying to laugh.

He hoped killing her with kindness was the way to get free, either by earning her trust or by her letting her guard down. "That's nothing, shortly after that I made friends with one of the chickens. Every night I would sneak her into the house so she could sleep in a little bed I made for her next to mine. My dad was so mad at me but my mom convinced him to let it be. I named her Penelope and shared a room with her every night for almost two years. Dad said we were the worst farmers he'd ever seen. Sadly, poor Penelope was older by then and we had to let her go."

Filip sighed heavily as he thought back on his pet chicken. A movement out of the corner of his eye had him looking over at the troll. She had reached up and was wiping tears from her eyes. He was more confused than ever at just what kind of troll she was.

Chapter Five

H enrik paced the horse stall he was supposed to be cleaning. Fear for Filip was making him crazy. He hadn't thought Filip's plan was that dangerous but now he was regretting not siding with Jakob and refusing to let him go. He leaned over the divider and waited for Jakob to stop shoveling and look up at him. "It's been nine days; we should have heard something by now."

Jakob sighed heavily. "I'm afraid you're right. I knew I shouldn't have let him go."

Henrik went back to pacing. Jakob's agreement didn't make him feel any better. "Let me go see if I can find him. I'll stop along the route and see if anyone saw him."

Jakob stopped and walked to the divider between them. "I think one of us needs to go towards the bridge."

Henrik froze. "You really think he went that way?"

Jakob nodded; his mouth drawn in a grim line. "I think we have to assume that's why we've not heard from him."

Henrik didn't want to admit out loud how much the thought scared him. He'd heard of so many people not returning from that area. If his brother went that way, then he was surely lost to them and Henrik was terrified whoever followed Filip would be next. Henrik cleared his throat and straightened his shoulders. He was going to do what a good brother should. Protect Jakob. "I'll leave immediately. If I get near the bridge and he wasn't spotted along the route I'll come back here before going the other route."

Jakob threw his shovel against the wall and walked around to the other stall. He grabbed Henrik and hugged him tight. "Don't take any risks. If you get to the area and people say they saw him, come get me and we'll cross together." He waited for Henrik to agree with a nod. "Now go find our brother and bring him home."

Henrik swallowed past the lump in his throat and hurried to the house. He packed light and tossed some food in his bag before going to see his parents.

He knocked quietly on their bedroom door before entering. His mother sat in the chair staring out the window. The soft snores from his father in bed were comforting to hear.

Henrik walked over and kneeled next to his mother. Her tiny hand reached up and cupped his cheek. "Have you word from Filip?"

He shook his head. He hated seeing the fear and worry in her eyes. "I'm sure he's so caught up in his work he forgot to send a letter. I'm going to be gone for a few days. I'll make sure everything is all right and then I'll come right home."

Silent tears rolled down her cheeks. He could see the distress in her eyes and felt the emotion down to his bones. He kissed her cheek and left. As he closed their door quietly he said a silent prayer they would still be alive when he returned... if he returned.

***

Henrik couldn't ignore the anger building inside him. He was well down the path leading to the bridge and his worst fears had been confirmed, Filip had taken this route. Multiple people confirmed seeing him. When he found his little brother, he was going to wring his neck for taking this risk.

In the distance, the opening to the bridge came into view. The horse stepped sideways, resisting moving forward. Henrik didn't blame the creature. He felt the tension in the air, too. But what options did he have? It was more than a day's ride home. Did he go back and get Jakob or go forward and have faith in himself... an image of his helpless parents lying in bed made the decision for him. They wouldn't survive for days while both he and Jakob searched for Filip. That settled his decision. Jakob needed to stay at home and take care of their ailing parents.

"Forgive me, brother," he muttered as he nudged his horse forward.

With each step the horse took, Henrik's muscles tightened more and more. He sat straight, scanning the area, hoping he managed to keep his face blank, without emotions showing, so his fear wouldn't be evident. The horse's hooves hit the wood of the bridge. At the same moment there was a loud crack behind him. He squeezed his thighs and tightened his grip on the reins as the horse reared up on its back legs. Something grabbed his coat from behind and yanked him off his horse. As he flew through the air, he caught sight of something hairy just before he smacked against a tree and went down. Darkness overtook him and he fell unconscious.

Chapter Six

H enrik woke up and jumped to his feet, ready to fight whoever had attacked him.

"It's okay, she's gone."

Henrik froze, did he recognize that voice? He felt around, his back was to a wall and he was surrounded by ropes on three sides. He walked carefully to the side he heard the voice and peered between the ropes. "Filip, is that you?" Henrik squinted trying to see who was in the makeshift cage a few feet away.

Filip sat against the back wall of his cage and waved. "Yeah, I was taken before I could even cross the bridge. Are you okay? What about Mother and Father?"

Henrik circled the enclosure, yanking on the ropes of his enclosure. "We're fine, it's you we were worried about."

Filip didn't look his brother in the eye. "I screwed up; I know."

"Hey." Henrik waited until Filip looked at him. "I don't care about any of that. You're alive and that's all that matters."

Filip nodded and smiled. Henrik knew he didn't need to ride his brother. Filip was already paying the price for his choice. "By the way, did you say *she*?"

Filip chuckled. "I'm ninety percent sure it's a she. It's a troll of some sort but she acts so human that I'm not totally sure."

Grunts from the front of the cave stopped their conversation. Henrik watched the large, hairy creature walk in dragging a doe behind it. The troll laid the doe by the fire then grabbed a piece of rope and walked over to Filip's cage. Henrik was going to yell at the beast to stay away but stopped when he saw the smile on Filip's face.

His brother stood still and let it tie his feet with a small bit of rope between them. His jaw dropped open as he watched Filip follow the troll over to the fire and sit next to it.

Filip pointed at Henrik. "That's the one I told you about with the turkey."

A scratching noise from the troll perplexed Henrik. He could see its shoulders moving up and down. "Is it laughing?" Did he mutter to himself?

Henrik was fascinated watching Filip mindlessly chatter to the troll as they cleaned and cooked the deer. Every time Filip grabbed the knife, Henrik thought Filip would use it to fight for their freedom but instead, he cut meat and kept working. "Why am I not surprised you made friends with your captor?"

The troll picked up a rock from the ground and

threw it at Henrik. He backed away so it wouldn't hit him. Who knew it would be so touchy?

Filip scowled at him. Henrik didn't know what to make of their friendship. He sat against the wall and studied the creature. He agreed with his brother that it was likely a *she* and she was unlike any troll Henrik had ever heard of.

He was stunned when she got up and brought him a piece of tree bark with a pile of meat and berries on it. She put it between the ropes and held it out to him. "Thank you." She nodded and turned to walk away. "I won't put up a fight if you let me sit with you guys."

She snorted at him then went and sat beside Filip. She pointed at Henrik, then Filip, then back to Henrik.

Filip glanced at his brother then back to her. "You want another story?"

The troll nodded as she picked up her makeshift plate and started eating.

Filip stared into the fire for a few seconds before smiling and turning back to her. "When I was maybe twelve I went with my family to the market. We were walking around and I happened to see one of the girls from the farm next to us being picked on by these other two boys. They had taken her basket and were refusing to give it back. They kept threatening to dump the bread rolls out, she was crying and desperately trying to get it from them. Like usual I marched over there without any backup and demanded they give her the basket.

They were shocked for about five seconds then they tossed the basket towards her and turned on me. I realized my mistake too late as they grabbed me by the arms and ankles and started dragging me into the trees." Henrik smiled at the memory of what was coming. "They tossed me to the ground and one was pulling his fist back to hit me when they were suddenly yanked away from me. I jumped up and found Jakob and Henrik pinning the boy's arms behind their backs. I followed along as they dragged them over to a pig pen and threw them in the center of the mud. I found a bucket of slop and tossed it over them so the pigs ran over to eat. It was awesome watching them squeal and push their way out of the pen. They ran out of there and never bothered us again."

The troll held her belly as she laughed loudly, or at least that's what Henrik assumed she was doing.

They finished eating in silence then she walked Filip back to his cage. After she undid the rope at his feet he pointed at Henrik. "He always travels with books. If you have his satchel that was on his horse, he would probably love to have them."

The troll glanced at Henrik, then walked out of the cave.

Henrik stomped to the side of the cage facing Filip. "What are you doing? You had so many chances to attack her and now you're asking for my books like we're moving in here."

Filip crossed his arms over his chest. "I'm killing

her with kindness. She's done nothing to hurt me and has actually taken really good care of me. There is something about her that I haven't figured out yet. Either way, I'm hoping eventually she'll see we're not a threat and let us go." He pointed at Henrik. "And I wouldn't get any ideas about fighting her when she does take you out for bathroom breaks. She could crush your skull with her bare hands so don't tempt her."

Henrik wanted to argue but the troll returned with his books in hand. He was hoping she would bring the whole bag; he had a knife in there. She shoved the books between the vines and waited for him to grab them.

He stepped forward and took them. "Thank you." She grunted as she pointed to the book and then to him. "What?" She did it again.

Filip smiled. "I think she wants you to read to her."

The troll nodded eagerly. Henrik scowled at Filip for the suggestion. "Fine," Henrik growled, "but I hope she likes poetry because that's what I brought."

He sat down and leaned against the ropes so the fire would be behind him to cast enough light to read the words. "This has got to be the weirdest thing I've ever done."

A rock flew across the cave and hit him in the back. "Okay, I'm going, patience."

He flipped to the first page and forgot about everything around him as he got lost in the words.

Books were his solace; it didn't matter what was happening around him. As long as he had a book to read, he could survive anything.

Chapter Seven

Henrik yawned and stretched as he sat up. It had been two days since the troll had taken him. They had gotten into a rhythm. She would be gone for long periods during the day. Sometimes she would come back with gear from the King's guards and sometimes it was with animals for them to eat. Each meal she let Filip sit with her but she still didn't trust Henrik enough to let him out. That frustrated him because he had been on his best behavior since she'd brought him his books.

He walked to the door of his cage and glanced around, noticing both Filip and the troll were gone. Panic set in, he yelled Filip's name over and over again until the duo came shuffling into the cave as fast as Filip's bound ankles would let him.

Filip's eyes were wide with panic. "What's wrong? What happened?"

Henrik reached through the vines and pulled him against them to hug his brother. "I thought she had taken you. Normally I hear you when she takes you out."

Filip hugged his brother back. "I woke up early

and was struggling to sleep. I asked her if there was somewhere she could take me to bathe and to my surprise, she led me to a pond. It was only waist deep but it was enough to get the job done. I honestly couldn't stand the smell of myself any longer."

Henrik nodded his agreement. "We're both getting a bit ripe aren't we." He stepped back and looked at the troll. "I wouldn't mind a bath either." She growled and bent to pick up a rock. "Hey now, I've read to you every time you've asked."

To his surprise and relief, she stood back up, her hands empty of tiny projectiles as she led Filip back to his cage. She walked back over to Henrik's cage with a rope and reached through the vines. He stood still while she tied his hands and ankles, and then he shuffled slowly out as she led him to the pond.

The water was a glorious sight after days in a dimly lit cave. He didn't bother to ask if she'd untie his hands. It was very obvious she didn't trust him. He walked into the water fully clothed and sat down so it came up to his neck. He didn't think he'd ever had a bath feel so good before today.

He glanced back and saw the troll sitting on the water's edge creeping closer to it until her toes were in it. He watched her smile as she wiggled them. She continued to confound him. Trolls are supposedly animalistic monsters that attack without reason. She most definitely thinks and feels.

He dipped below the water one final time before getting up and walking out. She jumped back as he approached. "Thank you for letting me do that, I appreciate it very much."

Standing a foot away from her in broad daylight he could see the intelligence in her beautiful green eyes. If he ignored the rest of her body, he would almost think she was a human.

She yanked the rope and led him back to the cave. He didn't care that she offered no towel to rub the moisture off his body. The water cleaned him and had felt good, and that made it worth the time it'd take to drip dry.

He didn't put up a fight as she put him back in his cage. He waited until she had walked away before stripping down to his underwear. He laid his damp clothes over rocks jutting out of the cave wall.

A gurgling noise behind him made him turn around. The troll stood at the doorway staring at him. It was hard to tell in the firelight but he swore he saw her eyes travel up and down his body. "Go ahead, take a look. I am your prisoner after all."

She reached between the vines with something in her hand. He stepped forward and grabbed a book. It wasn't one of his. "Now, where did you get this? Did you go shopping for me?" *Progress.*

She snorted then surprised him when she sat on the ground and leaned against the cage door. When he just stood there staring at her, she grunted and pointed at him and the book.

He glanced up at Filip who shrugged, he seemed as surprised as Henrik was.

Not having anything better to do he sat on the other side of the door, turned to page one, and started to read. After a couple of pages, he heard her sigh as she snuggled against the vines and listened to him. Filip was right, she was no ordinary troll. It was up to them to figure out why she was different and why she was all alone in the middle of the forest without the rest of her kind.

Chapter Eight

J akob stood in the center of the potato field. Instead of harvesting the vegetable, he was staring off into the distance, willing his brothers to ride into view. It had been four days without a word from Henrik or Filip. He knew deep in his soul that something had happened to them and it had to do with the bridge he had told Filip to stay away from.

He knew he had no choice, he had to go after them. He couldn't wait and continue on like everything was fine. Their mother had gotten weaker by the day, worrying herself to death and he couldn't let that continue to happen.

He tossed the basket he held onto the ground and went to saddle his horse. It was a short ride to the next farm over.

He knocked swiftly on the door hoping someone was home and not all out in the fields working.

The oldest of the five daughters opened the door and he smiled politely at Ann Hansen. "Morning Jakob, how are you?"

Ann was seventeen and beautiful with her golden hair and blue eyes but Jakob had never been interested in her. As much as both their parents wished for the match there would never be anything between them. He just didn't feel anything for her. "Morning, Ann, is your father home?"

She held the door open and waved him in. "He's gone into town for the day. Is something wrong?"

Ann's mother, Mrs. Hansen, walked out of the kitchen, drying her hands on a towel. "Jakob, are your parents all right?"

The fact that she knew to ask that question was a punch to the gut. He hated that everyone knew how weak they had grown. "I've come to ask for your help. Filip went missing while looking for work, then Henrik went to find him and hasn't returned. I was hoping you could spare one of your daughters to stay with my parents so I can go look for my brothers. I've made sure there's plenty of food while I'm gone."

Ann grabbed her mother's arm. "I'll do it, mama, I'm happy to go take care of them." She smiled shyly at Jakob.

Mrs. Hansen nodded. "Of course, we'll help out. When should Ann go over?"

Jakob let out a huge sigh of relief. "I'm leaving within the hour. Thank you for your help."

Mrs. Hansen put her arm around Ann's shoulders. "Your parents will be well taken care of. I hope you find your brothers safe and sound. Godspeed."

Jakob nodded and left before they could see the tears well up in his eyes. His logical side insisted his brothers were dead. But he hoped he'd find them alive. *I will find them and bring them home safely either way. A burial is better than not knowing.*

As he rode home, he contemplated what he would say to his parents. How could he look them in the eye knowing he let something happen to his brothers?

He packed quickly and then left his bag by the door as he went to visit with his parents. He knocked and then entered. His father sat up in bed and crossed his arms over his chest. He scowled at Jakob. "Well?"

Jakob stood at the end of the bed and stared down at the blanket, not meeting his father's gaze. "I've arranged for Ann Hansen to look after you. I'm going to find Filip and Henrik and bring them back to you."

He straightened his shoulders and lifted his gaze to his father's eyes. For a few seconds, neither said anything. Finally, his father nodded. "I know you will; take care and come home quickly."

Jakob walked around the bed and kissed his mother's cheek. He was thankful she didn't speak or he wouldn't be able to control his emotions. Upsetting his father was one thing; breaking his mother's heart would be unbearable.

He closed their door quietly and gathered up his bags. He was halfway to the barn to saddle a fresh horse when Ann rode up. He held the horse's reins while she climbed down. He helped her take the tack off the animal before leading it into an empty stall. Neither spoke as they worked. He didn't want to give her any hope of there being something between them.

Once they were done, he led his horse out of the barn while Ann followed behind him. "Thank you," he said, glancing her way, "again for doing this. I know I don't need to worry about them while I'm gone."

Ann blushed. "I'm happy to help and my sister, Marie, will come over during the day to help me with the animals while you're gone."

He climbed on the horse. Ann reached up and gently touched his knee. "Safe travels."

He cleared his throat, uncomfortable with her touching him. "Thanks. I'll return as soon as I can."

Without a backward glance, he rode off toward Cressian Bridge.

The hours alone wondering what he was going to find would test every ounce of strength he had.

***

By dinner time the horse was exhausted and Jakob's stomach growled in protest. He'd pushed hard all day hoping to get to the bridge early the next day. He stopped at an Inn and paid the stable boy to take care of the horse while he went inside to get a meal.

The Inn was dark and mostly empty. The barmaid waved him in. "Sit wherever you'd like."

Jakob grabbed a table near the fire and waited. He looked around the room knowing it was stupid but still hoping to see one of his brothers.

The barmaid walked up with a pint of ale. "Can I get you a plate of food?"

Jakob nodded. "I'll take whatever I can get with this." He handed her a few coins and ignored the pity he saw on her face. She turned to leave but he held his hand up. "Also, my brothers may have come through here over the last fortnight. Filip and Henrik both look like me but a bit younger. They were heading for Cressian Bridge perhaps?"

The young woman clucked her tongue. "I remember one of them coming through and asking about the other. I hadn't seen the first one but one of the other customers had. After a quick meal, he kept going. I haven't seen either of them come back through, though."

Jakob sighed heavily. "At least I know I'm on the right path."

She patted him on the shoulder. "I'll get your meal."

Jakob took a long swig of the ale. It didn't sit well in his stomach.

It didn't take long for the girl to return with a large plate of chicken and potatoes. He stared down at the food. "Surely, my money won't cover all of this."

She glanced over her shoulder toward the door

to the kitchen. "Not to worry; I've got you covered." She turned to walk away and he reached out and grabbed her wrist. She gasped and pulled her arm away, cradling it against her chest. Her sleeve had pulled up just enough to see she was already bruised from something else. "I'm sorry; I didn't mean to hurt you. I just wanted to thank you. I know everyone is having a hard time right now."

She smiled sweetly. "Don't worry about me; I can handle myself. Now, eat up. You have a journey ahead of you." She started to walk away then turned back again. "I hope you find your brothers."

Jakob nodded, then pulled the plate closer. The truth was written all over her face. She wasn't okay and she didn't think his brothers were either. He couldn't save everyone right now. He had to focus on his brothers. Together they could find a way to help the girl who risked her own safety to make sure he was taken care of.

Chapter Nine

J akob straightened up in his saddle as he
approached the bridge. He studied the
ground and searched the woods hoping
to see his brothers or their horses. At the entrance
to the bridge, he paused. Something shiny off to
his left caught his eye. He dismounted and tied his
horse to a tree to look around the woods a bit
more. Not that he expected to find a trail of items
leading to his brothers but he couldn't ignore
anything out of the ordinary.

He shuffled through the fallen leaves of the
forest until he found the object that had caught his
attention. "What the hell?" A shield from the King's
guards leaned against a tree. "Why the hell is this
out here?"

As he bent to pick up the shield, a putrid smell
engulfed him just as the ground beneath him
shifted and he was lifted into the air and trapped
inside a web of vines.

He kicked and thrashed, yelling for help. The
ropes were so tight he could barely move. He heard
someone walking through the leaves behind him.
"Hello, is someone there? Can you help me?"

Whoever was there didn't say a word. He felt his bindings being shifted before he was dragged across the forest floor. He yelled and fought as hard as he could but all he could see were the trees and sky above him. He ignored the pain every time his body went over a rock or large stick. He would kill whoever captured him when they removed the restraints.

Eventually, his view darkened as he was dragged into a cave. His captor pulled him into another vine structure. He felt movement by his feet and then another sound he couldn't identify before silence.

"Jakob, is that you?"

Tears sprang to Jakob's eyes. "Filip?" He glanced about, frantically trying to find his brother.

"I'm here, too," Henrik's voice came to him in the dark.

Given his current predicament, Jakob shouldn't have laughed but he couldn't help it. Relief swept through him that he found them alive.

"You can get up, she's gone." Henrik said.

Jakob tested his feet and found that the enclosure had been cut open. He squirmed out of the vines and threw them across his cage. He ran to the side of his enclosure and saw his brothers in similar cages. "I can't believe you're both alive! And did you say *she*?"

Filip chuckled at his brother's indignation. "Well, it's a troll. Henrik and I are convinced it's a female."

Jakob glanced around the cave. He took in the large pile of bones near the fire pit and the mound of swords and shields. "Has she been eating soldiers?"

Filip shrugged. "Not that we've seen. She's actually keeping us well fed but it's mostly been rabbit and deer."

Henrik was quick to chime in. "Are mother and father okay?"

Jakob nodded. "I left Ann Hansen with them. They will be taken care of until we get out of here. What have you tried so far?" Henrik smirked at Filip who scowled at him. "What, what am I missing?" Jakob asked, feeling his forehead crease with his scowl of confusion.

Henrik chuckled before filling him in. "We think the troll likes Filip. She still gives me my food in the cage but she ties his ankles and lets him eat by the fire with her."

Jakob scowled at his little brother. "You've been making friends with a troll while I've been worried sick about you?"

Filip grabbed the vines and leaned against them. "I'm truly sorry but she cries every night and I can't explain it but I think she's starting to say words."

Jakob glanced over at Henrik who nodded in agreement. "It's true; I've heard them, as well. I'm not convinced she's a troll but, if she's not, I don't know what that makes her."

Thunder rumbled loudly, echoing through the cave. Lightning lit up the entrance outlining the troll as she came in dragging a deer behind her.

Jakob studied the creature hoping to find some weakness they could exploit so they could escape and return home.

The cave was silent other than the storm raging outside and wet sounds of her gutting the deer. The three brothers watched as the deer was drained and skinned. The smell of cooking meat wafted through the cages. Jakob couldn't deny she moved like a human. She skillfully cooked the meal and brought a piece of tree bark over with a pile of meat on each and slid them between the vines to him and Henrik. She walked over to Filip's cage. Her gravelly voice came out as a whisper. He strained to make out what she said. He thought she said, "Feet."

She reached between the vines and tied his ankles together before opening the door to let him out. Filip glanced at his brothers and smiled before following her over to the fire. Jakob ate while he watched his little brother bond with their captor.

Filip sat on the ground and faced the troll. "You can speak now? You know my name is Filip and that is Henrik. Your newest catch is Jakob. Do you have a name?"

The troll froze then looked up and studied each of them. She turned back to Filip and nodded. For several seconds she made several strange sounds before managing to growl out "Amalie."

Henrik gasped. "As in Princess Amalie?"

Chapter Ten

T he troll jumped up, grabbed a handful of gravel and rocks, and threw them at Henrik. She made a choking sound, then grabbed Filip and pulled him toward his cage. She shoved him inside and stormed out of the cave.

Filip grabbed the vines and stared at his brother. "Did the troll really tell us she was the supposedly dead Princess?"

Henrik paced his cage. "If that's true, the King has a lot to answer for."

Jakob shrugged. "Unless he doesn't know. Maybe she was kidnapped and turned into a troll."

Filip quirked an eyebrow. "You mean the King who's starving his subjects?"

A gasp by the cave entrance had them all turning. The troll stood there staring at them. "Starving?" she croaked out.

Filip nodded. "The Kingdom is in ruin. Your father has lavish parties while his people ration their food."

Jakob walked closer to the door of his cage. "Did your father do this to you?"

The troll nodded as she sat by the fire and cried.

Filip's heart broke for the girl. He'd never seen her in person but he'd heard she was as beautiful as she was kind. "What about your mother? We were told you both died in a carriage accident."

The Princess sniffled as she wiped her cheeks. "Mother died but I survived. They took me to the castle because I was hurt," her voice cracked as she spoke. Filip assumed she hadn't spoken in the year and a half since she'd been turned. The three brothers stayed quiet and let her take her time getting the words out. "Father couldn't bring himself to order my death again. He sent for a sorcerer who turned me into this and then they threw me out here in the woods to fend for myself."

Filip's heart broke for the girl. First, she lost her mother and was almost murdered by her father, then she was turned into a troll and dumped in the woods. "I'm so sorry that happened to you; you didn't deserve it."

Jakob nodded. "It's impressive really. I'm sure most royals wouldn't be able to survive, let alone thrive out here. You've done an amazing job."

Amalie snarled at him. Filip rolled his eyes at his oldest brother. He always was a little clueless about other people's emotions.

Henrik sat on the ground and stuck his face between the vines. "May I ask, why are you keeping us alive? Why not kill us like you have been doing to the soldiers."

Everyone turned and looked at the pile of swords, shields, and helmets.

Amalie shook her head. "I've not killed anyone. The King sends them here to spy on me and make sure I'm still here. I catch them, steal their stuff, and then leave them to return to the castle with their heads hung in shame. I have no idea what story they are telling my father about what happened to them."

Filip laughed loudly. "I doubt they are admitting you're kicking their asses."

"I don't care what they tell him. I'm waiting for the day he comes looking himself and then I'll be ready to kill him."

Chapter Eleven

F lames danced in Amalie's eyes as she stared at the fire. She wasn't ready to look up at the caged men and see the horror on their faces. She couldn't really blame them; not many people would openly admit they were going to kill the King. She wished she didn't care what the three beautiful boys in front of her thought but unfortunately, she did.

When she was first turned, she was more troll than human. In the first couple of months, she didn't know who she was or that she could even speak. It took months of spying on people for her memories to start returning but even then, she'd had no will to do anything about it.

Then two weeks ago she saw Filip riding toward the bridge. Her past came into focus, she knew exactly who she was and what had happened to her. Thanks to the beautiful boy she had purpose again. She didn't know what she was thinking when she decided to capture and keep him, she just knew she wanted him.

She spent days outside the cave practicing speaking. Her throat burned at first but she pushed through and kept repeating phrases her tutors had taught her. When she finally spoke again, she wanted to sound like a princess but the grating sound of her voice was proof she was never going to be that girl again.

Shame had her storming out of the cave. Now that they knew who she was, she didn't want to face them like she was.

She marched over to the pond and waded in. She didn't care how long it was going to take, she was going to scrub her body until she no longer smelled like a swamp creature. As she sat there running her fingers through the hair on her body, pulling the knots apart she couldn't help laughing as she remembered the exact moment she became aware of her own smell. It was just after Henrik's bath, she had sat next to his cage and when he sat down she caught his scent, it reminded her of sandalwood and musk. Then when she shifted to get comfortable, she caught her own scent which reminded her of a rotten animal. It was the first time since being turned she was actually embarrassed.

***

Amalie walked back into the cave with her head held high. Her hair was dry and knot-free. It was the closest she would likely ever come to feeling human again.

The three brothers openly stared at her. She

hadn't realized how badly she had stunk until now. Not that she had cared before now. She was pure animal until they had woken up her human side.

Filip smiled at her. "You look like you had fun. We would have swam with you."

She shrugged. "Maybe next time."

Jakob cleared his throat. "We're sorry for everything that happened to you but our parents are sick and we had to leave them to find Filip. Can you let us go so we can get back to them?"

Guilt engulfed her that she had been keeping them because she was lonely and all this time their parents were home worrying about them. Thanks to Filip's conversations and Henrik's stories she had been able to reclaim more of her humanity and understood she needed to let them go. "I'm sorry, I didn't mean to keep you from your family." She twisted her gnarled hands as she rushed over to their cages. "I don't know why I caged you. You are free to go to them." She opened Filip's cage and undid the ropes she had left on his ankles when she had stormed off earlier. She glanced at him and gave him a small smile before moving on to Henrik's cage. She opened his door and stepped away quickly. She paused at Jakob's cage. "Please don't hurt me for taking you and your brothers."

She opened his cage door and scrambled back by the fire. Trolls were stronger than humans but, now that they knew who she was, she didn't want to use it against them. For a brief period, she had wanted to be close to them and feel human again. Sadly, it was time to let them go.

It didn't matter what she used to be. It only mattered that she was a smelly, hairy, beast that lived in the woods. What could she offer these handsome boys?

Chapter Twelve

Filip hated the idea of leaving Amalie but he needed to see his parents. It had been almost three weeks since he'd left. He had to see for himself that they were okay, then he would come back for her.

Amalie followed them out of the cave. "Your horses are tied up just over that ridge. I've been making sure they were taken care of."

Jakob nodded. "I appreciate that. We don't have many animals to spare." He took off in the direction she had pointed. Henrik bowed to Amalie then took off after his brother.

Filip reached for her hands, but then pulled back. They had never touched before and she was the Princess. A peasant shouldn't touch royalty but he saw the hurt in her eyes. "I promise to return and help you. We need to check on our parents but then I'm coming back and we're going to make a plan to get you out of this."

Tears welled in her eyes. "There's no plan to make. I can't challenge my father like this." She handed him a large sack he hadn't noticed before. "Take this deer meat for your parents and tell them

I'm sorry for keeping you from them." Filip grabbed the heavy bag. It was illegal to hunt in the King's woods. If they were stopped and found with this they would be arrested. Then again, it was more than enough to feed his parents for weeks, and maybe that would help them get on their feet again.

"Filip, let's go," Jakob yelled as he ran to the top of the ridge.

Filip looked back at Amalie. "I will be back."

He took off after his brothers. As he crested the ridge, they were already on their horses and waiting for him.

Jakob tossed the reins to Filip's horse to him. "If we ride through the night, we can be back late tomorrow. Do either of you have money still?" Henrik and Filip nodded. "Good, there's an Inn a little ways back. We'll stop and get some food so we have it for the ride."

Filip sighed heavily as he mounted the horse.

Henrik walked his horse over to Filip. "Smile, we're going home."

Filip straightened up and smiled at his brother. "I'm good, I promise." How could he tell his brother he had started having feelings for the troll before he ever knew she was the Princess?

***

As soon as their farm came into view, all three brothers kicked their horses into a run and took off for the house.

Ann stood on the porch watching them ride in. Filip had always admired her beauty and sweet temperament but now that he had spent time with Amalie, he knew it had been nothing but childhood infatuation.

Jakob dismounted first and started undoing his tack. Ann waved him off. "Your parents have missed you. Go see them and I'll take care of the horses."

Henrik shook his head. "That isn't fair. Filip, you go first and we'll join you as soon as we're done here."

As Filip walked by Ann he squeezed her shoulder. "Thank you for stepping in while we were gone. You saved our family."

A blush spread across her cheeks. "It was nothing really; it was a nice change for me and your parents are the sweetest people."

He made his way up the steps. Behind him, he heard Ann gasp. "We can't take this. What if it's found?"

"Look how much we have here," Henrik said. "There's more than we could possibly eat before it spoils."

Filip chuckled as he walked through the door. He had no doubt hunger would get the best of Ann and she would take the meat to her family.

His hand shook as he reached up and knocked on his parents' bedroom door. Fear threatened to paralyze him, he wasn't sure what to expect. How much worse would they be since leaving almost a month ago? "Mom? Dad? We're home."

Filip's mother leaped from the bed with more energy than he expected her to have and launched herself into his arms. He held her as she wept against his chest. "It's okay, Mom, we're safe."

His father walked over and wrapped them both in a hug. No one spoke for a few minutes until Henrik and Jakob joined them. Their father walked over and cupped Jakob's face. "I knew you would bring them back. You're a good boy."

Henrik wiped a tear as his mother kissed his cheeks repeatedly.

Filip was grateful they looked no worse than when we had left them.

Their father walked back to the bed and sat down. "Now, tell us where you've been."

The three brothers exchanged looks. How did they even begin to tell the story?

Filip rubbed the back of his neck before finally blurting out, "The supposedly dead Princess who had almost been murdered by the King is now a troll and kidnapped us. She let us go when we told her about you and now here we are."

Chapter Thirteen

Their parent's mouths hung wide open, their eyes round with disbelief.

Henrik shook his head. "Jesus, Filip, you could have taken that a bit slower." He looked back at his parents. "And honestly, I think she let us go because she's sweet on Filip."

Filip rolled his eyes at his brother. He knew the Princess would never have feelings for a farmer, let alone a third son. He wasn't even worthy of working in the palace, so there was no way she could ever feel anything for him. "Regardless of the why, I need to go back. I have to help her. She doesn't deserve to live that way. She should be ruling the Kingdom."

Their father scoffed. "And just what do you think you can do for her?"

Filip shrugged. "I'm going to help her take down the King."

His mother gasped and covered her mouth. Filip knew what he was risking but they weren't going to be able to talk him out of it.

Jakob rested a hand on his shoulder. "I agree something must be done but I don't think we're the people to do it. We have no power."

Filip walked over and kneeled in front of his mother. He grabbed her hands and pleaded with her. "She had to watch her mother be killed, then she was turned into a troll when she survived the accident. She is living in a cave, alone, and constantly watched by her father's men. You taught us to do what was right and to help people. I can't leave her there."

She reached up and brushed a lock of hair off his forehead. "You've always been so compassionate. This bravery is a nice surprise. I'm proud of you for risking everything to do what is right. We'll be fine while you're gone but you come back to us."

He kissed her cheek, then stood up and kissed his father's cheek. He turned and found his brothers staring at him. "I'm sorry, I have to go."

Jakob shook his head. "Can we at least talk about this first? Let's weigh our options."

The idea of wasting time, hashing out plans with them while Amalie was in her cave feeling abandoned, made his skin crawl but he owed it to his brother to not be rash again. "What do you propose we do?"

The room was silent as everyone considered what their next move should be.

Henrik sighed. "What if we told people what happened. If enough people get upset, the King will have to address it."

Jakob shook his head. "As soon as word got out that we were spreading this rumor, we would be silenced and likely in the permanent fashion."

Filip nodded in agreement. "Not to mention the story is so insane I doubt anyone would believe us."

Jakob stared out the window for a second. "And I suppose just marching her up to the castle gate wouldn't go over well?"

Their father chimed in. "If the King has people watching her, they would kill you all well before you arrived at the King's gate. No matter what plan you come up with, it will require Amalie to be a part of it and you're going to need to be as stealthy as possible up to the last second."

Their mother sat forward. "I think any plan you try to make will struggle to work as long as she is the way she is. Why not find another sorcerer to reverse the curse?"

All four men turned and stared at her. Filip walked over and kissed the top of her head. "Do you think it could be reversed? Regardless, it's the logical next step. Does anyone know how to find a magic person?"

Everyone fell silent again.

Filip shrugged. "It's okay. I'll ask around while I'm headed back to Amalie and, who knows, maybe she knows where to find one. If we get stuck, I'll bring her back here with me. I'm not leaving her alone again."

His mother blew him a kiss. "Be safe my love and take care of the Princess."

***

Filip was exhausted, he'd not slept more than a couple of hours in the last few days. He wanted to get back to Amalie and let her know she wasn't alone. He rode straight for the cave, surprised when he didn't see her in the forest.

He tied up the horse and walked quietly into the cave.

His heart broke as he followed the sound of crying and found her lying by the fire sobbing. "Amalie, don't cry."

She gasped as she sat up, wiping at her face. He knelt in front of her. It was the first time he was close enough to see the hazel color of her eyes.

"Why are you here?" she asked, staring at him with red-rimmed, wide eyes of disbelief, like she was surprised to see he actually returned as he'd promised.

He shrugged, as he smiled. "We have a Kingdom to overthrow, don't we?"

She glanced down at her body. "I already told you, I can't lead like this."

He held his hand out. "I know and that's why we're going to find our own magic person to see if they can turn you back."

Her hand shook as she reached up and put her gnarled hand in his. He didn't shudder or pull away. She smiled at him, he hoped she understood he wasn't disgusted by her.

He helped her up. "Pack what you need. I stopped

at a tavern nearby and heard about a sorceress a day's ride from here."

Amalie glanced around, looking at the home she had built over the last year and a half. "I don't really have anything I need to take with me."

Filip couldn't imagine how it felt to go from being the Princess living in a castle to having nothing. For her sake, he hoped when they got back, her father hadn't gotten rid of all of her stuff. She at least deserved to have a picture of her mother.

Hand in hand they walked out. Amalie paused at the entrance and said, "It's different walking out for what may be the last time."

Filip squeezed her hand. "We'll get you home, Princess. Let's go."

He pulled a cloak from a bag tied to his saddle and handed it to her. "We're going to stay off the road as much as possible but I think you need to stay hidden."

Amalie adjusted the cloak so nothing but her hands and feet showed. If she hid them, no one would know a troll rode a horse while in the company of a man.

Filip climbed onto the saddle and then pulled Amalie up behind him. He chuckled quietly.

Amalie nudged his shoulder. "What's so funny?"

"Three weeks ago, if you told me I'd be here right now, searching for a sorcerer and trying to overthrow the King, I wouldn't have believed you."

Amalie giggled. "Most fairy tales, the knight in shining armor rides in to save the day. I guess we did it backward with me kidnapping you first. However, you came back and that means everything to me."

As the night wore on, they talked quietly about their childhood and their families. It struck Filip how different they were yet felt so comfortable together now. Amalie might have grown up with everything she could ever want but Filip felt like he was the rich one for having an entire family who loved him unconditionally. Amalie had only had her mother and even then she often sided with the King over her.

As the sun rose through the trees, they found a small pond surrounded by thick trees. "Let's get a few hours of sleep, then we'll start moving again when the sun starts going down."

Amalie slid from the horse and stretched. Filip jumped down and untied a bundle from the saddle. "Do you want to start a fire while I make us a place to sleep?"

She bounced on her toes. "I'll do you one better. I'll go catch a rabbit and make food, too."

Filip's stomach growled in response. It still felt strange being able to hunt and eat without fear of arrest.

He tied several pieces of cloth between a few trees and laid down a large pad for them under the shade.

"Foods done, come join me."

Filip sat by the fire and grabbed a handful of berries Amalie had picked. She handed him a stick with pieces of meat on it. He bit into the first bite and groaned. "Did you know how to cook before all of this happened?"

She shook her head as she chewed. "Not really. I'm an only child, so I did sneak into the kitchen occasionally just to be with other people. I guess I picked up some stuff. Trust me, the first couple of months out here I thought I would die of starvation. It took a while for me to learn how to hunt. I threw up the first few times I prepped the animals for cooking."

Filip tried to picture a troll gagging as it cleaned out a deer. The image had him laughing until tears rolled down his face.

Amalie elbowed him. "Don't laugh, I was literally a spoiled princess before that. I think I managed quite well, thank you very much."

Filip held his hands up defensively. "No argument there, you caught my brothers and me. I can confirm you are stealthy."

Amalie took a small bow. "Awe shucks, that's not a compliment I ever expected to receive."

Filip tossed his stick into the fire. "Well, I don't know about you but I could use a bath." He winked at her before walking over to the pond and kicking his boots off. Inside his stomach was in knots but he tried to act calm as he tossed his shirt off and then his pants. He might have imagined it but he thought he heard a gasp behind him.

The cool water slightly stung against his skin as he walked in. He flipped on his back to float and glanced out of the corner of his eye. Amalie stood on the water's edge twisting her fingers together. She was nervous and he wished to put her at ease. "You can join me, I won't bite. Plus, we both know you could kick my ass if I tried."

Amalie chuckled, then walked in. "How deep is it? I don't know how to swim."

Filip put his feet down and stood up. "The water stops at my chest so you'll never be underwater. I'll be here in case something happens, though."

They stared into each other's eyes as she walked towards him. She stopped a foot away from him, the water brushing her chin.

It sounded crazy but Filip wasn't seeing a troll any longer. He moved closer until they were near enough their breaths mingled. He'd never kissed anyone before, and as he leaned in, he wondered if she had.

A noise beyond the tree line had them jumping apart. "Someone's coming, get behind me."

Amalie raised an eyebrow at him. "I thought we already discussed who the stronger one was."

Filip laughed. He wasn't embarrassed by that fact. "Valid point, but how about we face them together?"

Amalie smiled and stood next to him in the water. Side-by-side they were ready to face whatever came their way.

Chapter Fourteen

Amalie was never nervous when she faced off against someone. She knew her troll strength would help her best nearly any human. It was different, though, with someone else to protect and she suddenly had something worth fighting for.

Now that she knew what her dad was doing to the Kingdom, she was more determined than ever before to stop him. It didn't matter how many guards were sent after her. She'd take them all down.

Two riders broke through the tree line and one of them called out, "Well, don't you two look cozy."

Filip rushed out of the water. "Jakob, Henrik, you came? What about mom and dad?"

Amalie followed him out of the pond but stood awkwardly off to the side. She hadn't bathed since turning, but when the brothers came into her life, she decided to get herself cleaned up. But when she did, she was alone so she would shake off like an animal. She could imagine their horrified stares if she did that now. She was going to have to wait it out and hope all her hair air dried quickly.

Henrik bowed to her. "We came as fast as we could. It wasn't easy following your trail but lucky for us, not many people go through this part of the forest thanks to the Princess' prowess."

She blushed at his praise.

Jakob nodded his head to her before looking back at Filip. "Ann is taking care of our parents again. Their family was very grateful for the food we shared with them and once we filled them in on what was happening, they told us to take as long as we needed. They are going to talk to the rest of the neighbors and together they'll take care of the farm, too." He glanced back at Amalie. "They understand the importance of what we're about to do and support you completely."

Tears filled Amalie's eyes. Her love of the people was part of the reason her father wanted her removed. As she got older, she had tried taking a more active role and her ideals for their people didn't align with her father's. "I promise to reward all of you when I become Queen." No more *ifs*, but *when*. Her people needed her.

Henrik tied his horse next to Filip's, then walked over to the fire. "So, do we have a plan yet?"

Filip nodded eagerly. "We're keeping Amalie out of sight as much as possible, so we're going to sleep for the next few hours and then ride through the night again. By tomorrow morning, we'll be at the home of a sorceress I was told about. We are going to break the curse; then we need to visit the villages and let them see their Princess is alive and let her tell them her story. Once we have enough people behind us, we'll march to the castle."

Amalie was awed at his loyalty and willingness to fight for her. "Actually, I think we need to be stealthier about going to the castle. I think I can sneak our group inside undetected. We'll have the villagers start gathering in small groups around the castle. By the time the guards figure out they are congregating as a mob, it will be too late."

Jakob stretched and walked toward his horse. "Before we get too excited about storming the castle, we need to make sure everything else goes right first. That starts with sleep and I've not had any in two days."

Amalie watched as he added a pad and blankets to the area Filip had already set up. She studied the oldest brother, fascinated by his serious nature. She had always wanted a sibling, an overprotective brother like Jakob, or maybe a sister who looked up to her. Either way, she loved watching the camaraderie between the siblings.

Filip cleared his throat. "That bed was going to feel much bigger when it was just the two of us, Amalic. Would you like me to make you a bed somewhere else?"

Heat rushed to her face as she realized what he was saying. He was giving her the choice of sleeping with three gorgeous men or all by her lonesome. "I'd rather stay close."

They both knew that was just an excuse, there was no reason for her to need to be close. He didn't mind though. His hand rested on her lower back as he led her towards the makeshift camp. She briefly wondered if he was disgusted by the hair all over her or the misshapen way her body was contorted. He didn't remove his touch as they crossed to the bed, so she assumed he felt the same pull to her that she felt toward him.

The brothers stood by and let her get comfortable. She didn't want to make anyone uncomfortable, so she chose the far left side. Filip laid next to her, then Henrik, followed by Jakob on the other end.

As she closed her eyes and listened to Filip's quiet snores, she said a silent prayer of thanks to fate for sending her own personal army.

With any luck, this time tomorrow she would be herself again and Filip could see her for who she truly was and not the gnarled monster he had to look at now.

Chapter Fifteen

"**A**malie, wake up, you're moaning in your sleep." Her eyes fluttered open and Filip leaned over her. "Were you having a nightmare?"

She rubbed her eyes as she sat up. "Yeah, I think so, but I don't really remember."

No way was she going to admit she was most decidedly not having a nightmare. Quite the opposite, actually. In her dream, she was herself again and the three brothers were in bed with her. They took turns kissing, touching, and making love to her. Or at least what she imagined would happen in bed. She was still a virgin, so she relied on her extensive reading knowledge and vast imagination to fill in the blanks.

"Henrik, enough of that, help us pack up." Jakob untied one of the tarps Filip had hung above them.

Henrik sighed as he closed the book he was reading and put it in his bag. Filip had mentioned they were farmers. Amalie realized how close-minded she was to find it surprising a farmer would be carrying books and reading them. Not that she thought they were stupid in any way but many of her staff couldn't read so she assumed most people who did manual labor were the same. The lack of educational resources had been part of her conflict with her father and that was one of the few things her mother had sided with Amalie on. She wanted to expand education for all of their citizens, not just the ones who could afford to send their children to school.

"Amalie, do you think you could catch us a few rabbits to cook before we get moving?" Filip stood over the fire, building it back up.

She hopped up, eager to help in any way she could. No one would arrest a troll for hunting, so it made sense for her to take the risk. Not to mention she was pretty damn good at it, too.

When she returned with three large rabbits, the camp was packed up and the guys sat around the fire waiting for her. Her breath was robbed from her as she looked at them. Each gorgeous in their own way and all willing to risk their lives for her. It was truly the first moment in her life she didn't feel alone. Even when she'd been a princess in the castle, she'd been lonely.

All three stood when they saw her. As had become their custom, Jakob nodded to her, Henrik bowed, and Filip's smile curled her toes. She handed Filip the rabbits and sat down next to him. She was hyper-aware of the hair covering her body and the knots and twists contorting her normally curvy body. It took every ounce of willpower to continue sitting there acting normal, when inside she was so self-conscious, she wanted to run away and find a cave to hide in.

As Filip cooked the rabbits over the flames, he kept glancing over at her until she finally looked up at him. "You've probably met a lot of royals and aristocrats growing up in the castle. Anyone truly bizarre?"

Jakob snorted and shook his head. "You don't know your place, do you? You can't ask those questions."

Amalie put her hand up toward Jakob to stop him. "It's okay. We're all friends here." *Nothing like being turned into a troll to automatically put you in the friend zone.* "When I was around fourteen, a group from Pillaney stayed for a week. The Prince was twenty, I believe, and full of himself. He had maids follow after him everywhere he went. Before he sat, he made them smooth down the cushions. They handed him everything, he never had to reach for a thing. I honestly don't know how he wasn't four hundred pounds from the lack of activity. My father had been hoping to marry me off to him, but, thankfully, my mother talked him out of it."

Henrik scoffed. "He sounds like a complete buffoon."

Amalie chuckled. "He wasn't the worst. When I was sixteen, the King of Gandria came with the hopes of securing my hand. He *was* four hundred pounds, and older than my father. He was a snob who didn't care about his people at all. He interrogated my mother about my health and brought a doctor with him who wanted to evaluate me to ensure I would be a good breeder."

Filip reached over and squeezed her hand. Amalie glanced down at his hand, then up at his brothers who both looked shocked that he was touching her. "No one deserves to be treated as an object for sale to the highest bidder."

Tears welled in her eyes. "We're royals, it's what's expected of us."

Jakob's eyebrows drew together, his mouth in a hard line. "If that's what royalty does to people, I'm glad I'm a poor farmer. I'll take my family, friends, and hard work over those imbeciles any day."

Amalie's hand shook as she covered Filip's, then she looked at each one before speaking. "You should be proud of the men you are. It's obvious your parents raised you well and I for one think you are worth more than every royal I've met combined." She reached up and wiped a tear from her cheek. "Now, can we eat and get on the road? I'm ready to take down the patriarchy."

***

Amalie's stomach was in knots, they'd ridden all night and finally made it to the supposed magic person's house. The single-story home in the middle of the forest should have stuck out as odd but it looked like it grew there as part of the woods. As they tied their horses to a tree, Amalie noticed a garden on the side of the house nearly as large as the building it grew next to.

Jakob held his hand out to stop Amalie when she started to march to the door. "Perhaps let us start the conversation. Most people aren't going to react well to a talking troll no matter how well-spoken you are."

Filip rested his hand gently on her lower back. "I agree with him, let us check it out first. We're not even sure this is the right place."

Amalie nodded and pulled the cloak further over her head. "I'll stay with the horses until you call for me."

She stood back and watched the trio walk to the door. Jakob knocked, then stood back. Amalie didn't know what she had been expecting but a beautiful brunette in her thirties wasn't it. Her anxiety built as the guys took turns speaking but Amalie couldn't hear what was being said.

Finally, Filip turned and waved her forward. She held the cloak tightly closed as she approached. The woman smiled at her. "Don't be afraid, child, I can see the magic around you. Your aura is a mess."

Out of nowhere tears poured down her face. The woman held her arms out and wrapped Amalie in a hug. It was the first hug she'd received since losing her mother. She held on and let go of all the pain and anguish that had been bottled up for the last year and a half.

When her tears were spent, she pulled back, embarrassed at how long she had held on to the stranger. Amalie turned around and found the brothers had walked away to unsaddle the horses and brush them down. She appreciated that they had given her a few moments of privacy to have a breakdown. "I am so sorry; I don't know what came over me."

The woman waved her off. "I'm used to it; you could say it's one of my gifts. People feel comfortable around me and often end up confessing more than they want to." The older woman searched Amalie's eyes. "So, it's true, you're the Princess?"

Amalie shrugged. "What's left of her at least."

The woman stepped back and held the door open. "I'm Berit and I would be honored to help you if I can." She leaned out the door and yelled, "Come in and join us for tea when you are finished."

Amalie studied the house as she was led through a sitting room into a dining room. She would never have guessed this woman was a sorceress. There was no giant cauldron bubbling over the fire, or bats hanging from the ceiling.

Berit leaned close and whispered in Amalie's ear, "Not what you were expecting?"

Both women laughed as Berit held out a chair for Amalie. "I don't mean to stare; I've got little experience outside of the castle, so I really didn't know what to expect."

Berit filled a kettle with water and put it on the stove. "So, do you remember the sorcerer's name who cursed you or what he looked like?"

Amalie fidgeted with the lace edging of the

tablecloth trying to distract herself from the pain of the memories. "I was badly hurt when they brought him in. I never caught his name but he was in his sixties, maybe, with long gray hair that curled past his shoulders. His eyes were so brown they were almost black."

Berit filled two cups with water and put pouches of leaves inside each cup before placing one in front of Amalie. "I'm not surprised he would go along with the King's plan. The sorcerer you were so unfortunate to run into was Matthias. He only cares about making money from his powers. Greed will be the end of him one day. Magic doesn't like to be taken advantage of."

Amalie shivered at her words. She'd always heard there was a price to using magic but Berit made it sound ominous.

A soft knock on the door had both women turning to watch the three brothers stroll inside.

Berit stood up and grabbed three more cups. "Let me have a look at you." She studied each one for a few seconds. "Okay, have a seat. Your tea will be right up." Filip's eyes widened and he gave Amalie a panicked look. She shrugged and held her cup up to him. They each took a seat and watched Berit as she took small amounts of leaves from various jars and made each guy their own unique pouch, then put them in the cups to steep. She set them in front of each of them. "Now, wait five minutes before drinking. Let the leaves do their magic."

Amalie glanced down and studied the contents. She had just drank without even questioning what was inside it.

Berit sat quietly looking at each of them. The tension in the room was palpable as each person stared at their drink like it was about to start talking or something. Berit burst into laughter. "I'm just teasing you. I promise there is nothing in your leaves that isn't completely normal. You don't have much experience with the magic world, do you?"

All four shook their heads. Amalie smiled sheepishly, embarrassed to be so naive but glad she wasn't alone. "Is sorcery a family business?"

Berit took a sip of tea before answering. "Not that I'm aware of. My parents don't approve and think it's the devil's gift; so, I left their judgmental house and have been out on my own ever since."

Amalie felt like she had found a kindred spirit. Both women fighting to be who they were with parents who disapproved.

Berit reached out toward Amalie. "May I read your palm?"

Amalie was embarrassed to put her grotesque hand into the soft hands of the other woman but she didn't feel like this woman judged her in the least. She laid her hand palm up and watched Berit lean closer and study it. The sorceress's thumb lightly brushed against the fine hair covering Amalie's palm as she studied the lines underneath. "Interesting."

She turned to Filip. "May I?" He wiped his hand nervously against his pants, then laid it in her hand. "Mm-hmmm."

Without saying a word, Berit turned and waited for Henrik to let her study his palm next. "I see."

She turned to Jakob with her hand out. He stared at her, his jaw tensing until he finally sighed and laid his hand in hers. After a few seconds, she sat back and smiled at them. "It's as I expected. You have quite the journey ahead of you. It will take all four of you in order to restore the Princess to her rightful place."

Amalie pointed at her chest. "But what about my appearance? You can change me back, right?"

Berit shook her head, pity in her eyes. "This magic is tied to your father's hatred for you. If your mother were alive, I believe her love for you could break the curse."

Tears welled in Amalie's eyes. The sorceress' words were a knife to her heart. "I'm alone in this world with no one who loves me so I'm cursed to remain this way forever."

Amalie couldn't breathe, the pain was too much. She shoved her chair back and ran from the house. The whole idea had been stupid and never had a chance. She just wanted to go back to her cave and forget she ever had dared to hope for a cure.

Chapter Sixteen

Amalie ran through the forest, uncaring that it would take her days on foot to make it back to the cave. She just wanted to go home.

She barely heard the crunching leaves behind her or Filip yelling her name. He grabbed her arm and pulled her to a stop. "Let me go, we tried and we failed, it's over."

Filip held up his finger as he bent over to catch his breath. Amalie couldn't help but laugh. Trolls were stronger and bigger, so, naturally, she could run faster than him. She was impressed he managed to catch up at all.

"Phew, okay, I can breathe again." He wiped the sweat from his forehead. "If you want to go back to the cave, we can do that. I'll go wherever you ask me to. Or you can come home with us, my parents would be happy to have you."

Amalie's eyebrows pinched together. "What about the Kingdom? I thought you wanted to save it?"

Filip shrugged. "We'll find another way to take down your father. Now that we know what he's done, we can't look the other way. But, if you don't want to be involved, we'll come up with a new plan." He stepped closer and reached up to cup her face with his hand. "I have feelings for you, I don't know what they mean yet but I can't deny they're there. You tell me what you want and I'll make it happen."

Amalie's heart beat so fast, she thought her chest would explode. This sweet man, with nothing to offer, didn't care about what she looked like, yet he still treated her like she was beautiful. Ignoring the fear of rejection always bubbling up inside of her, she reached forward and kissed him. For a second he froze, his eyes wide as he stared at her, then he turned his head and kissed her back. His arms wrapped around her, she felt cherished for the first time. His mouth tentatively opened so she followed suit. She didn't know what she was doing but she didn't care. She was going to follow her gut and do what felt right.

They finally pulled apart, breathless with need.

Filip's eyes widened, he stepped away from her. "Jesus, Amalie, look at you!"

Amalie glanced down, thinking something was on her. A blonde lock of hair fell in front of her eyes. She reached up and gasped as she realized her long, blonde curls had returned. She studied her body. It was still covered in hair but she'd shrunk back to her normal height. "It's happening... oh my god, my voice is back to normal."

She fell against Filip and sobbed with relief. He ran his fingers through her hair as she cried.

When she had nothing left except hiccups, she stepped back and looked down at her body again. "Why didn't I shift all the way? Why did it stop?"

"Maybe we didn't do enough. I'm willing to kiss again for the sake of the curse, of course." He winked at her.

"Very cute, let's go see if Berit has any answers and if she doesn't, we'll go with your plan."

They walked hand-in-hand back toward the house. Filip kept glancing over as they walked. "It's so strange to have to look down at you now. You're so tiny."

"Are you looking at the same body? I may have gotten shorter but nothing else about my body has gotten smaller."

Jakob and Henrik froze when they caught sight of the couple walking back into the clearing. Amalie's cheeks heated feeling their gazes on her. Berit came out of the door with a huge smile on her face. "I admit, I thought it was going to take a bit longer."

Amalie ran up to her and whispered. "Why did it stop? We kissed and I changed but not all the way. Do I need to sleep with him for it to complete?"

Berit leaned in and whispered back. "While I wholeheartedly approve of you enjoying yourself with him, I'm not sure that will help. All I can tell you is that you are on the right path and need to keep moving forward. Come with me." She looked at the brothers still staring in shock at Amalie. "We'll return shortly."

Amalie followed Berit through the house to a bedroom. She walked over to a mirror and stared at herself. It was the first time she'd seen her face since the carriage ride. "Oh my god, I'm hideous. How can he love me like this?"

Berit picked up a brush and pulled it through the long curls. "You have a very special young man. He sees you for the woman you are on the inside. Sadly, there aren't many men like him in the world."

Amalie's hand shook as she reached up and stroked her cheek. She struggled to comprehend she was the creature looking back at her.

Berit finished brushing her hair, then walked over to a closet and pulled out a dress. "In case you do shift further you should start wearing clothes. If you lose the hair on your body you are going to expose more of yourself to the Kingdom than you probably want to."

Amalie giggled at the image of "the Princess" standing in all her naked glory in the middle of a town square while begging her people to follow her in a revolt. "That would be one way to get my father's attention, though I agree that probably isn't the wisest plan."

Berit handed her the dress. "Not everyone is as accepting as we are, so it's best to present the most royal image we can in the hopes they can see past the curse." She grabbed a pair of shoes, then looked at Amalie's feet which were still disfigured and put them back in the closet. "I mean, really, a talking troll should be enough to convince them but some people are a bit dimwitted."

Berit packed a few more dresses in a satchel then opened the bedroom door. "Let's go see your man."

Amalie's hands were fisted at her side as she walked back through the house and out the front door. She stared at the ground as she walked toward the brothers. When Filip's feet came into view she glanced up. He smiled at her. "Lovely, as always." He leaned forward and kissed her gently.

She glanced at Henrik who bowed and Jakob who nodded. She appreciated that they didn't make a big deal out of the kiss.

Jakob grabbed the satchel from Berit and tied it to his horse. "Are we continuing on to the village, your Highness?"

Everyone held their breath waiting for Amalie to make the decision. The next move they made would alter all their lives. Whether it would be for the better or worse no one knew for sure.

Amalie turned and hugged Berit before stepping toward Filip. "Let's go save my Kingdom."

Chapter Seventeen

Henrik didn't want to admit it but he was nervous. Of the three brothers, he had always been the shy, introverted one. Now they were about to walk into town and start talking to strangers and convince them of a crazy plot against the King.

Jakob pulled his horse to a stop. "The village is just ahead. Why don't we make camp here? Two of us will go on and see if we can find anyone to listen to what we have to say. If we can get a group together, we'll bring Amalie in to speak to them."

Filip looked over his shoulder to talk to Amalie. "Do you mind staying here with Henrik?" He glanced over at his brother. "No offense, but you aren't the most dynamic speaker and I think this is going to take some finesse."

Henrik let out a long sigh. He wanted to hug his brother for understanding. "None taken, it would be my honor to watch over the Princess." There, that sounded manly.

Amalie smiled at Henrik. "Of course, I'll stay with you. Maybe we can get more reading in."

He slid from his saddle and tied his horse to a

tree before walking over and helping Amalie down from Filip's horse. He reached up and patted Filip's back. "Good luck, I hope you return with good news."

He grabbed the bags from Filip and Jakob's horses then watched them ride off. Once they were out of sight he turned to Amalie. "I'll start setting up a sleeping area if you want to get a fire going?"

She nodded and went to gather wood. They worked quickly and had everything set in record time. Henrik realized he should have taken his time, now he had nothing to do but talk to Amalie.

She sat by the fire and patted the blanket next to her. "Come rest for a while."

Needing a distraction, he walked over to his bag and grabbed a book before joining her. They sat in awkward silence until Amalie turned to him. "There's no nice way to say this so I'll apologize now. I am fascinated that you are such an avid reader. There were only a handful of servants in the castle who could read." She gasped and grabbed his arm. "Not that I'm calling you a servant. I was told that school is only for those that can pay and I guess I assumed you probably spent your days working on your farm?"

Henrik glanced down at the warm hand on his arm. He reached up and covered it gently. "You are quite right; we couldn't afford the time or money for school. However, the wife of the family next to us is a teacher. At night she would teach the girls, and offered to let my brother's and I join in. My father agreed as long as it didn't impact our work on the farm."

"That's one of the points I argued with my father about. I wanted free school for all children but he disagreed. I have so many ideas on how to help the people and my father was against every one of them. He wants his people under his thumb at all times. I guess my ideas were so radical he decided murder was the only option he had." She cleared her throat and blinked away tears.

"Have you thought about walking away? You could live on the farm with us, we'd find a way to make it work?"

She stared off into the woods then straightened her spine and shook her head. "I believe this is my purpose. I have to correct the wrongs committed by my father. My life isn't my own, it belongs to my people." She gave him a small smile and shrugged. "Anyways, I've always enjoyed reading. It was the one thing my mom always made sure she did with me. When it was time for bed she would come in and read me a story. I think that's partly why I am so connected to books; they remind me of my time with her."

Henrik absentmindedly stroked the top of her hand with his thumb. "For me, it's about escaping. I can't control my parent's slowly starving to death, or the amount of never-ending work there is to do on the farm. But for me, at least for a couple of hours a day, I can read a book and imagine I'm in some far off land or in a place where the bad things in the world don't exist."

"Would you mind reading to me now, let's escape somewhere together?"

***

Dinner was ready as Filip and Jakob rode back into camp. They tied up their horses and joined Henrik and Amalie at the fire. Filip leaned down and kissed Amalie. Henrik was surprised to feel jealous. Today was the first day they had to relax and he hadn't even noticed she had ensnared him under her spell too.

Jakob grabbed the plate of food Henrik held up to him. "That went better than expected. The Innkeeper agreed to let us meet in their private room at eight o'clock. People want to believe it's true but until they see proof they aren't going to stand up to the King."

Filip swallowed a bite of food. "People are desperate for change. It's obvious just by looking at people they are starving and desperate for help. If we only talk to those who are most in need, we should be able to fly under the palace radar for a while. These people know their neighbors, they'll know who they can share the plan with and who they can't."

Henrik smiled at the excitement on Amalie's face. She set her empty plate down. "Do you think there will be enough people, can this actually work?"

Everyone turned to Jakob, being the oldest they had unconsciously made him the leader. He chewed his food for a minute not speaking. Henrik knew he never made any rash decisions. This was his way of taking his time and thinking through every step. "I do think it's going to work but we need to be methodical about it. We'll identify the strongest in every village and send them the soldier's gear from the cave. Once we've gone through every town, we'll plan a strike and send runners ahead to each town with the date and time. We'll send our soldiers toward the palace and have them try to get inside at the same time we sneak in. Hopefully many will get in before it's figured out. While the castle is focused on the extra troops and us, they'll not notice the mob growing and surrounding the outer walls."

Henrik had to admit the plan sounded good. He was proud of his brother. They were out of their comfort zone and doing their best. Jakob was handling this like a seasoned soldier.

Filip set his plate down and stood up. "I think it's the perfect plan." He reached down and held his hand out to help Amalie up. "If you're finished eating you have an audience with your people."

***

Henrik stood next to Amalie with Filip on her other side. Jakob stood right in front of her. Between the three of them and the cloak hiding her no one would know what she was. They were positioned outside the back entrance of the Inn waiting for the owner to let them in.

Amalie had a death grip on Henrik and Filip's hands. "Do you think anyone will show?"

Jakob turned around and faced her. "Even if it's only one person that's still one more who will know the truth and fight for justice."

Amalie took a deep breath and straightened her shoulders. Henrik was in awe of her strength. At eighteen she shouldn't be dealing with curses, dead mothers, and dethroning father's but she took it in stride.

The door creaked open, a weathered man in his sixties peaked out. "We're ready for you."

Jakob went in first, followed by the trio. Henrik was struck silent at the sight in front of him. He nudged Amalie, "Look."

She peaked around Jakob's shoulder and gasped. The room was packed full of people with only standing room left.

Jakob and Filip walked forward and stood on the boxes the owner had used to make a platform. Jakob waved his hand in the air to quiet everyone down. "Thank you for coming tonight, I understand the risk you are taking. We promised you proof that Princess Amalie was still alive and cursed, so without further ado here is your future Queen, Amalie."

Henrik squeezed her hand and walked her to the center of the makeshift platform. She had her head bowed at first but then she straightened up and pulled the hood of her cloak back. As expected, everyone in the room gasped and started speaking at once.

Amalie took the cloak off and handed it to Henrik. "Good evening, I'm sure this comes as quite a shock to all of you. What you've heard from the Gruff brothers is true. Your queen was murdered and when I managed to survive, he had me cursed and tossed into the woods to fend for myself."

She looked every bit a Queen standing there. Henrik could see the tension in her shoulders and her hands balled into the skirt of her dress.

Amalie glanced down at Henrik then back at the crowd. "My father doesn't have your best interests at heart. I want to take his place and make our Kingdom strong again. No one should be suffering while he entertains. We've come up with a plan and need your help. If we don't stand up together and demand justice, we'll all lose in the end."

The crowd cheered and stepped closer to the platform. Henrik's skin crawled with having so many people circle them. He slipped back by the door and let Jakob and Filip act as bodyguards.

***

As soon as they were outside again in the night air Filip grabbed Amalie and swung her around. The sound of her laughter had Henrik and Jakob pausing and staring at her. He didn't know about his brother but the sound sent a shiver of desire through him.

Filip kissed her lightly. "You were magnificent, everyone adored you."

Jakob grabbed the cloak from Henrik and held it out to Amalie. "Thanks to your speech we know exactly who we can send ahead with armor and who our runners are. Word will spread and this will be an epic battle your father will never see coming."

Henrik followed behind as they got their horses and made their way toward camp. He knew they were on the right path and doing what was best but he still worried something would go wrong and they'd never return to their parents.

Chapter Eighteen

J akob slid from his horse and bent her leg to check her shoes. "Well, damn. Henrik can you work the next village with Filip while I tend to the horses today." He fought the urge to roll his eyes at the look of panic in Henrik's eyes. "We all know I'm better suited for this particular job. Let Filip do most of the talking and you'll be fine."

Henrik sighed as he nodded. "You have done the last five villages so it seems fair I take over." Jakob noticed the longing look he gave Amalie. It hadn't slipped his notice that they had grown fond of each other over the last week. He wondered what they did all day hiding in camp while he and Filip talked to the villagers.

Filip punched Henrik lightly. "You and me, bro, let's do this." He turned and gave Amalie a kiss then helped her down from the horse.

She squeezed Henrik's knee as she walked by. "I'd wish you luck but you don't need it. You'll be fine." She grabbed the bags from his horse and walked over to Jakob.

As his brothers rode off, Jakob realized this

was the first time he would spend alone time with Amalie.

They worked quietly side by side as they set up camp and got the fire started. He grabbed the small tool kit he packed and prayed it would do the job since they didn't have money for a professional.

Amalie followed behind him and watched his every move. The silence was killing him. "Have you been around horses much?"

She reached up and let the animal sniff her hand. "I'm a proficient rider but usually they are saddled and ready for me and then taken care of when I'm done. I admit I've never watched what goes on when caring for one."

Jakob cleaned out the hoof he was holding. "What about pets? Did you have a dog or a cat?" From everything he'd learned from her so far, he had figured out she had been lonely. He hoped she at least had a pet to keep her company.

She shook her head. "My father had a few hounds when I was young but once he stopped sport hunting, he got rid of them. There was a barn cat that I think belonged to one of the stable boys. I would pet it sometimes when no one was around."

"Your life wasn't ever your own was it?"

She shrugged but didn't answer.

He moved on to the next hoof. "There's something that's been bothering me. When I was young, I remember the villages flourishing, our farms were growing crops in abundance. Everything started changing a couple of years ago, then drastically in the last year and a half. Besides you pushing for change, it seems like something bigger happened?"

Amalie absently pet the horse as she thought about it. "I believe he's got the early stages of senility. More and more frequently I would see him forget someone's name or the word for something. My mother was always quick to cover it up but being called the wrong name a few times when you're an only child tends to stick with you. His paranoia had gotten worse just before the accident. He had railed at my mother one night that he feared I was going to come for him while he slept. It wasn't just me though, he was growing more fearful of everything."

Jakob stopped working to look at her. "That is huge. Regardless of what he did to you, he's not fit to rule. Why aren't his advisors doing anything?"

Amalie snorted. "They are likely treating him like a puppet now, pulling all the strings and living lavishly while he deteriorates. All of his family is gone, I'm not sure what their plan of succession is."

Jakob was floored, it was so much worse than they had first thought. Feeling the weight of her declaration he wanted to lighten the mood. "We don't need to worry about his succession plan because you'll be in charge. What's the first thing you're going to do when you're Queen."

She tapped her finger to her lips as she considered the question. "I've always thought the castle was dull. Maybe I'll have it painted bright pink, inside and out, and the surrounding walls. Ooh, I could change out the guard's uniforms for pink ones too"

Jakob's jaw hung wide open. Of all the things he thought she would say, that was not one of them.

She threw her head back and laughed loudly. "I'm just teasing you. How vapid do you think I am? Seriously though, we have to fix the food supply issue first. I can't say how until we see what's been going on and where the issue is."

Jakob was impressed. Not many young people would be as logical and pragmatic as she was being. "Well, let's not throw out the pink idea completely. I think my brothers would look good in bright pink."

Amalie gasped. "The always serious Jakob made a joke? Not bad."

He shrugged as he turned and went back to working on the horse.

She stepped close to him. "In all seriousness though, I appreciate you being here. I know I can depend on your strength and leadership to get us through this. Filip is funny and loving, Henrik is poetic and deep, but you are my rock."

Jacob's throat went dry. She already had two brothers in love with her, he couldn't be a third. He wouldn't do that to either of them.

***

The sun was setting as Filip and Henrik rode into the camp. Amalie jumped up from the blanket and ran to greet them. It hurt Jakob's heart to watch her kiss Filip and hug Henrik.

Jakob handed them each a plate of food. "How did it go?"

Henrik sat down with a heavy sigh.

Filip chuckled as he sat next to him. "Well, I have good news and I have bad news. I'll start with the latter. Henrik is terrible at this job and I forbid you to partner me with him again. The good news is word spread ahead of us so people were already prepared when we started our speech. And even better, the Innkeeper offered us two rooms free of charge."

Amalie gasped. "A real bed, no hard ground? Tell me you aren't just teasing me." She leaped toward him and hugged him

Filip hugged her back. "If I had known it was that important to you, I would have thought of it sooner."

She turned and smiled at Henrik and Jakob. "Eat quickly now, there's a mattress waiting for me."

Jakob didn't have the heart to tell her it likely wouldn't be much better than the ground. She was too happy and he wasn't going to ruin that for her.

The foursome ate and packed up quickly. They

had become a cohesive unit over the last couple of weeks. It didn't take long for them to set up or break down.

They rode to town; Amalie kept her cloak pulled low until they got to the Inn and a large crowd was gathered in front trying to get inside.

Jakob pulled his horse to a halt. "Should we be concerned?"

Henrik shook his head. "No, this is the crowd we talked to earlier. As Filip said, they had already heard quite a bit so they were ready for us. They are all eager to meet their Princess."

A hush fell over the crowd as they took notice of them. Jakob rushed to get off his horse when he saw Amalie slide down and march toward the group. There was no way to be sure everyone there was on their side. All three brothers quickly caught up to her and flanked her, one on each side and one behind her. Now that she was human-sized again they dwarfed her.

As she walked, she pulled the hood down and ignored the gasps of shock that they had all gotten used to hearing when she first revealed herself. She stopped a few feet away and lifted her chin high. "I'm looking for people to follow me in a revolution. We have to end my father's reign and right what he's done to all of you."

Jakob studied the crowd. He watched as their expressions turned from shock, a bit of fear, to acceptance and then anger at the king. It always amazed him how fast people fell in line when they saw the talking troll for themselves.

Amalie continued on. "I want to hear from you, tell me your grievances about the King and hear our plan and how you can help."

The crowd ushered her into the Inn and led her to a table and chairs in the far corner of the dining room. Jakob sat to the side and listened as Amalie held court.

For hours she talked to each person and heard their stories and gave them promises of a better future. She spoke with her people until her voice was hoarse. When the crowd had slimmed down Henrik had grabbed a book and gone to sit in a different corner. Jakob didn't mind, he understood his brother needed the distraction to help deal with his anxiety.

Jakob watched Amalie stifle a yawn. He stood up and held his hands out. "I think that's enough for tonight. We appreciate everyone that came out but it's time for us to get some rest." He waved over the innkeeper. "Thank you for offering us rooms. We haven't had a decent sleep in a long time."

The elderly man bowed to Jakob then turned and bowed to Amalie, and Filip. Jakob could see his brother was as uncomfortable as he was with that action directed at them. "Of course, it is our honor to help in any way we can. My wife has left some food and drinks in the rooms for you as well."

Jakob yelled over to Henrik. "We're going up, are you coming?"

He held up his finger. "I'll be along shortly."

Everyone chuckled, they knew that could be a minute or an hour.

At the base of the stairs, Amalie paused. "Filip, can you ready my room for me. I'll be up shortly." She turned to the innkeeper. "What are the room numbers?"

He blushed at her undivided attention. "You're in room four your highness and the gentleman are in room six." She nodded and walked toward Henrik.

Jakob ignored the jealousy trying to overcome him. He was happy for Filip and even for Henrik who was getting more alone time with her.

Jakob and Filip followed the old man up the stairs to the last two rooms on the left. He was going to have to try to sleep without thinking about what was happening in the room next door.

Chapter Nineteen

Amalie walked over and pulled the chair out across from Henrik.

He glanced up then closed the book when he saw who it was. "Is everything all right?"

She nodded.

He glanced around and noticed they were alone. "Is there something you need?"

This was it; she was about to admit her feelings and they were almost as crazy as talking to a Princess who was now a troll. "Well, I have a bit of a problem and I'm hoping you can help me."

He set his book down, his eyebrows scrunched with concern. "Of course, whatever you need."

"Here's the thing, I have feelings for Filip." Henrik's shoulders slumped slightly. "I also have feelings for you." She wasn't ready to admit she also lusted after Jakob. "The more I think about what Berit said about us being on the journey together and me needing all three of you in order to take my place as queen, the more I think she means I need you intimately not just on a battlefield."

She sat back and watched his stunned face as he worked through multiple emotions. His mouth opened and closed repeatedly before he managed to get words out. "To be clear, you are saying instead of one woman and one man, you believe we are destined to be one woman and three men?"

She nodded. "I have an easy theory on how we can find out if I'm correct. If I'm right it should only take a kiss from you for me to shift more."

She tried to play it cool but she felt like there were tiny ants running all over her body. She prayed he didn't reject her.

He leaned forward but she pushed back. "I'd like a little more privacy. Why don't we walk upstairs and kiss by the rooms?" He grabbed his book and started to stand. She grabbed his hand. "I want to be clear that I won't choose between you. Filip is already waiting for me in my room but if this does work, I hope that means I'll get to spend tomorrow night with you." *Oh my god, did I just say that out loud? Who is this woman in control?*

Henrik pulled her up to him. "I've never had grand illusions of being in a relationship with a Princess. I know I'm beneath you and will be happy with any piece of yourself you are willing to give me."

She shook her head vehemently. "Being born into one family over another doesn't make anyone better than the other. I love you, but I also love your brother. It's not traditional but I hope it's one that will work for us."

He nodded and followed as she pulled him up the stairs. They stopped in front of their doors. She spun around and rested her hands on his shoulders. "It's going to be fine either way." She wasn't sure if those words were for him or for her. She refused to believe she was wrong and this kiss wouldn't break the curse.

He bent down and she reached up to meet him halfway. Their lips met, he turned his head to deepen the kiss, she sighed with pleasure until a tingling across her skin had her gasping and pulling away. She looked down and watched the hair on her arms fade away. She reached up and felt her face, it was glorious skin. Tears rolled down her face. "I knew it, I knew you were both meant for me."

Henrik stroked her cheek. "I can't believe it worked. I'm not sure how we'll explain the troll being gone to the next village but I'm happy either way."

She looked down and rubbed her hands down her body. "The troll isn't completely gone. This still isn't my body. It's kind of nice that you didn't notice."

He laughed as he bent down to kiss her again. "Because I don't care about your body. It's your mind, and soul that has captivated me."

Amalie sighed contentedly as they kissed again. She finally pulled away. "Do me a favor, don't tell Jakob. I want it to be a surprise in the morning."

Henrik bowed his head. "I'm yours to command."

She entered the room quietly, scared and excited for Filip's reaction. He was sitting in a chair in front of the fire watching the flames. When he heard the click of the door he stood up.

His mouth hung open, shocked at the change. He rushed over and cupped her face between his hands. "What happened?"

She grabbed his hands and pulled him back to the chair. "Sit so we can talk." She waited for him to sit then she shocked him by sitting on his lap. She wanted to be as close to him as possible as she tried to make him understand. "You mean everything to me. I was lost when you came along, and if it wasn't for you, I would still be trapped inside my own head not remembering who I was. I love you, completely and totally." He started to speak but she held her hand up to stop him. "But I also love Henrik."

"So, you kissed him and shifted more?"

She nodded, "I thought a lot about what Berit said and I had a suspicion all three of you were tied to me. I figured it was just a kiss so if it didn't work there was no harm done."

She could see the hurt in his eyes. "Does that mean you have to kiss Jakob too?"

She shrugged. "That's my suspicion but I don't know for sure. Will this upset you?"

Her stomach was in a knot while he stared at the fire. She didn't know what she would do if he rejected her.

Finally, he looked back at her. "I don't honestly

know how to feel about it. You're asking me to not only share you but share you with my brothers." He reached up and stroked the smooth skin of her cheek. "On the other hand, we can't get married anyway so I should be grateful for any time I get with you before it all goes away."

She turned into his hand and kissed his palm. "I know this isn't what any of us expected but we can't ignore the obvious. I don't want to lose you but I understand if you need time to think about it."

She stood up and walked to the window. She didn't want to watch him walk out the door and definitely didn't want him to see the tears pouring down her face. He had to make the decision on his own without any guilt from her.

She heard the click of the door behind her, it was a knife to her heart.

She hadn't heard him walk up behind her until his hands came up and rested on her shoulders. He reached up and brushed her hair off one shoulder.

Her tears of pain turned to ones of relief. The click of the door must have been him locking it. She leaned against him and tilted her head to give him more room to kiss. When his mouth touched the curve where her neck and shoulder met, it sent shivers down her body.

She reached behind her and cupped his ass, pulling him hard against her. She could feel his erection pressed against her lower back. He loosened the ties of her dress, letting it fall to her waist. As she turned around, she held it against her chest. "Do you mind dousing the fire so it's darker in here?"

Filip rested his forehead against hers. "If that is what you wish I will do it. However, I think you are gorgeous and I don't care that you haven't fully shifted back. I loved you weeks ago when you were still a troll from head to toe."

Amalie choked on a sob. He was right, he had always seen her for exactly who she was. "I don't deserve any of you."

He gently pulled her hands away and pushed the dress over her hips and let it pool at her feet. He backed her up against the bed until she was forced to sit down. He kneeled in front of her. "Let me show you what you deserve."

She never expected his words alone would be enough to make her wet but she felt the heat building between her legs. His lips trailed from her neck down to her breasts. She watched as he kissed and sucked them. He pushed her back and kissed further down. She had only read about the things he was doing to her and now she realized reading it doesn't even come close to experiencing it firsthand.

He lifted her legs and rested them on his shoulders. Her breath sped up with anticipation. He looked up and smiled at her right before his mouth covered her clit. She arched up at the intense heat but he pushed her back down. His tongue drew circles around her clit until she was grinding against him. The image of him feasting on her was almost as erotic as him actually doing it.

His tongue thrust inside her, she bucked against him but his arms locked her hips in place. She was unintentionally resisting the building orgasm but he was going to make sure she enjoyed every second of it.

He reached up and squeezed her nipples as his lips closed around her clit. Her hands fisted in his hair; she held his face against her as the crashing waves of her orgasm overcame her. At that moment she couldn't think about the man she was holding against her. All she could do was feel the intense pleasure rolling through her body.

As the feelings subsided, she collapsed back against the bed, out of breath.

He stood above her smiling, there was something satisfying about seeing his face and chin wet from her. "You look pleased. I hope that means you will sleep well tonight."

She shook her head at him. "I've no intention of sleeping yet. I want more of you."

He started to kneel again but she stopped him. "No, I mean I want you naked on top of me." She saw the indecision on his face. "It's okay if you're not ready."

He rubbed the back of his neck. "It's not that. I don't have any protection with me."

She sat forward. "I meant it when I said the three of you are part of me. I will not be marrying someone else. When I am Queen, I make the rules and my first rule is that I don't have to marry anyone. My children will be legitimate and I don't care which of you is their father." She could see she shocked him speechless. "I know it's radical and there will be people who don't agree but I believe if my people are well fed and taken care of, they will see past our family arrangement."

She reached up and undid the buttons of his shirt. "I believe in fate and destiny and if she says I should have three lovers I won't fight her on it. I'm leaving my life up to her. Now, get undressed and come to bed. We can sleep or we can do more, I'll let you decide."

She scooted back and laid against the pillows. Her nipples tightened as she watched him undress. Farm life may be hard work but it definitely did a body good.

He kneeled on the bed and crawled toward her. She hoped his erection was a sign that he wanted more. She opened her legs and let out a breath when he laid between them. She had no idea the weight of a man on top of her would be so satisfying.

His cock was nestled against her still wet pussy, she was resisting the urge to squirm. He kissed her softly as he adjusted his hips. He was on the verge of entering her when he paused. "Last chance, are you sure?"

She grabbed the sides of his face and pulled him close. "I'm with you until the end, we don't know what will happen tomorrow. I'm not living my life scared any longer."

He slid inside her and claimed her body and soul. She felt the pinch of her virginity for a brief second before pleasure overwhelmed her. He buried himself deep over and over again.

Amalie reached down and dug her nails into his ass cheeks. He hissed and sped up, the pounding rhythmic bump against her clit was too much. She squeezed around him and yelled out. He thrust twice more before coming with her.

She held him against her until he caught his breath. She wasn't ready for the moment to be over.

Filip cleared his throat and looked up at her. "Are you okay?"

She brushed the hair from his forehead. "It was perfect, you were perfect."

He rolled off of her and pulled her against him. "I still can't believe this is real life. Every night before I go to sleep, I say a prayer that it isn't all a dream and I'm going to wake up at dawn and work the farm." He kissed the top of her head. "I know you think we saved you, but the truth is you saved me too."

Amalie wiped a tear from her cheek. She loved this boy more than she thought possible. No matter what happened over the next few days she vowed to protect him and his brothers until her dying day.

Chapter Twenty

J akob heard muttering but wasn't ready to open his eyes. Amalie was right, the bed did feel incredible after all the time they spent sleeping outdoors.

The mattress gave way as someone sat next to him. "Ugh, fine I'll get up."

He rolled over and nearly jumped out of bed. "Amalie?" He glanced at Filip. "Jesus, what did you two do last night?"

Filip shook his head as he pointed to Henrik.

Jakob stared at Amalie's porcelain skin. "I don't understand, you were with Filip last night, weren't you?"

He saw both Filip and Amalie's cheeks redden. They definitely did something last night. He just didn't understand how Henrik was involved.

Amalie walked over and held Filip's hand then she reached over and grabbed Henrik's hand. "It's as Berit told us. You're all meant to be part of my journey back to the throne. On a hunch, I kissed Henrik last night and the curse broke more."

Jakob studied each of their faces, trying to comprehend what she was saying. "So, you think you have to be with all three of us in order to completely break the curse?" The trio shook their head in unison. "That's the most ridiculous thing I've ever heard. Who's ever heard of such a notion, relationships are supposed to be monogamous."

Amalie walked back to the bed and sat down again. "You can't refute the fact that I partially shifted after kissing each of them. Perhaps if you kiss me, I'll shift the rest of the way?"

He ripped his blanket off and yanked his clothes on. "This is crazy. Berit said love had to break the curse, I can't love you and you can't love all three of us. It's too much, I'm sorry."

He stormed out of the room, his heart racing as he stomped down the stairs.

The Innkeeper waved him over to a table laden with food. "I want you all to have a good meal before you move on to the next town."

Jakob wanted to storm out of the Inn and walk off his shock but he couldn't refuse the older man's offering. "Thank you, we appreciate it. And the bed was wonderful. It was the best sleep I've had in a long while." That was mostly true. It had taken him a long time to fall asleep. He kept picturing Amalie in Filip's arms and it made him crazy until he finally fell asleep from exhaustion.

He sat down and made a plate of food. Amalie and his brothers came downstairs and were ushered over to the table. He ignored them, he had no choice, their idea was preposterous to him.

Amalie thanked the Innkeeper as he pushed her chair in for her then walked away. "We need to take note of everyone who is going the extra mile for us. I want to make sure they are well rewarded when I'm in charge."

That gave Jakob an idea. "We've almost circled the entire Kingdom. The last town is the one just before the bridge where you were. There's a waitress at the Inn who fed me when I had no money and I saw bruises on her. Do you think there will be a place for her in the palace? Leaving her in that place has weighed heavily on me."

Amalie smiled brightly. "I think that is a wonderful idea and I would like to meet this girl when we get there and thank her for what she's already done for you."

He nodded and went back to eating. His mind still racing on the morning's revelations and what it could possibly mean for their future.

***

As the foursome rode into the last town they were greeted with excitement. The news of their plan had spread even faster than they had expected. Along the way, they had met a few people who were unhappy with them but mostly because they were scared to stand up and risk what they had. Jakob didn't blame them; it was a lot to ask someone to join a war and possibly lose everything. They had yet to find anyone sympathetic to the crown, people understood the gravity of the situation and were very careful with who they told.

The Inn's stable boy met them outside and offered to feed and take care of the horses. Jakob wasn't sure how Amalie was going to repay so many people back but then again just restoring the balance of the Kingdom would likely be enough.

Jakob paused at the entrance to the Inn. He was afraid the girl would be hurt worse or not there at all.

Amalie walked up and lightly touched his back. "I'm sure she's fine. It sounds like she's a survivor."

Jakob nodded and opened the door. Every person in the room stopped talking and turned to stare at them. Amalie had the cloak still covering her body as her form hadn't shifted yet but there was no doubt looking at her face and hair that she was the Princess everyone remembered.

Jakob let out a deep breath of relief as he saw the waitress walk out the kitchen door. Her face lit up when she saw them. She waved them forward and pointed to a long table along the wall. She curtsied to Amalie. "Your Highness, it's an honor to have you here." She turned to Jakob and waved. "I see you defied odds and found your brothers? I worried about you when you didn't return."

The kitchen door swung open; a large older man stepped out. "Mary, you're slacking."

Jakob's fist tightened as he took in the Innkeeper. With his beefy hands and the scowl on his face it was likely this was the man hurting Mary.

She bowed her head and turned to rush away when the man spotted Amalie. His expression didn't change but he rushed over to their table. He grabbed Mary's arm. "Why didn't you tell me they were here?"

Mary tried to hide the pain as she answered. "I sat them and was getting their drink order then I was going to get you. I thought it was most important to see to their comfort first."

Amalie stepped forward; her tone stronger than any he'd heard from her before. "Mary was an excellent hostess; we were grateful for the quick service after such a long trip."

The Innkeeper let go of Mary and bowed to Amalie. "I look forward to seeing you in your rightful place. What your father has done to this Kingdom is dreadful. I'm not sure how much longer I can stay open. Travelers don't come through here much anymore."

Jakob stepped forward, ready to show the man how it felt to be grabbed like he had Mary but Amalie reached back and held him still. She nodded at the Innkeeper. "I've seen firsthand what's happened to the villages." She turned and looked at everyone in the room. "I vow to make it right; we will restore our Kingdom to its former glory."

She stepped back and sat at the table. Jakob waited until the Innkeeper had walked away before sitting. "Why were you so nice to him?"

She placed her hand on his balled fists. "We're

about to go to war, we can't anger anyone and risk they tattle to the king. We'll get her out of here and fate will take care of him. She'll not spend another day in this Inn."

Jakob sat back and tried to relax as Mary walked back to the table. "I'm so sorry, I had to run some food. If you're hungry I'll bring four pints and a bowl of stew for each of you." She curtsied again to Amalie. "I hope our meager offerings will suffice."

Amalie smiled warmly at the girl. "You are doing wonderful and we'll be grateful for anything you can spare."

Mary's cheeks reddened at the praise. "Henry also wanted me to tell you he has his two finest rooms available for you tonight."

Amalie nodded at the girl and turned to Filip and Henrik. "Could the two of you go thank Henry and then you can take our belongings to the room? I'd like to speak with Jakob for a moment."

Jakob didn't like the sound of that but he knew he couldn't avoid alone time with her forever. Mary led Filip and Henrik to the bar then went to get Henry.

Amalie leaned in and spoke quietly. "Is the reason you are so resistant to being with me because you have feelings for Mary?"

Jakob's eyebrows scrunched together. The notion had never occurred to him. "I'm not trying to help Mary because I have feelings for her. I am trying to help her because she is being hurt and no one should be forced to stay in that situation." He sighed heavily. "Since you aren't going to leave it alone, I suppose we should discuss it. I do have feelings for you but so do my brothers and I'm not going to step on their toes. I'm going to ignore my feelings and focus on getting you on the throne then I'll go back to the farm and you can live happily ever after with one of them."

Amalie glanced around to make sure they weren't being listened to. "First of all, I love that you want to help her just because that's the person you are. Second, you are going to look me in the face and deny the logic that kissing two of your brothers partially changed me so it makes sense you are the final piece to the puzzle?"

His jaw tensed; he was frustrated she couldn't understand. "You are asking me to go against the person I am. I believe love is between two people, not four. I don't think I can share you."

It pained him to say it out loud. That was the crux of the issue. He loved her too much to share her. He wanted an all-consuming love filled with endless days and nights of passion. Not to be on a schedule getting affection from her when it was his turn.

Amalie opened her mouth to respond then stopped when Mary walked up with their drinks. "I'll be right back with your food."

Jakob saw Henrik and Filip standing at the bar, he waved them back over. He needed more time to think, any buffer he could get would help.

Filip searched Amalie's face. "All good?"

Jakob saw the love on her face as she looked at his little brother. "Yes, we're fine."

Both brothers turned to him and scowled. This was exactly what he meant; he didn't need extra people in his relationship.

Mary returned and set down bowls and two baskets of bread before curtsying and leaving.

They ate in silence; it was easiest since all eyes were on them. The room continued to fill as more people came to speak with the Princess. Jakob felt like they were on a stage, was this what it would always be like if he did stay with her?

Filip pushed his empty bowl away and set back. "Before Amalie speaks with everyone, we should decide the timeline. This was the last town so when are we going to strike?"

Henrik set his cup down. "I saw the King is having a party tomorrow night. With all of the guests coming in they likely won't notice the extra soldiers. We can lay in wait until the King is tipsy and confront him in his bedroom when he has the least number of guards with him?"

Jakob shook his head. "Amalie can decide but I think we need witnesses to his treachery. I say we sneak into the party and confront him there."

The three brothers watched Amalie as she considered the options. "I agree with Jakob, this needs to be public."

Filip shook his head. "I'm worried that isn't enough time to get everyone in place."

Amalie disagreed. "We've been preparing everyone as we go. The runners will take off in every direction and get people to the meeting points. With us encircling the castle, we don't all have to meet up at one point. While I'm talking to everyone can you and Henrik go and organize the runners, take them to the cave to collect the soldier's uniforms? Jakob can stay here and make sure both Mary and I are safe."

Jakob was pleased she asked him to stay. It felt good knowing she trusted him to keep her safe.

Filip squeezed Amalie's hand as he got up, Henrik touched her shoulder. There were too many eyes on them for anything more physical.

Amalie pasted on a bright smile. "Wish me luck."

Jakob sat back and settled in, the next few hours were going to be long but at least he got to spend the time watching Amalie and making sure Mary stayed safe.

Chapter Twenty-One

It had been a long day and Amalie was exhausted. She loved that her people were so passionate about how to fix the Kingdom but after three weeks of hearing it, she was growing antsy to start doing something about it.

She signaled to Jakob to help her wrap up.

He stood up and held his hands up to get everyone's attention. "Thank you all for coming. I'm sure you can understand we have a lot to do to get ready for Saturday so we hope you'll understand our need to call it a night."

Jakob sat back in his seat as everyone did as they were asked and bowed or curtsied to Amalie as they left.

Amalie waved at Mary. "Mary, can you come here please."

The young girl wiped her hands on her dress and rushed over, she curtsied as she got to them.

Amalie touched her shoulder. "There's really no reason to curtsy every time you come over. We're not formal here."

Mary's cheeks reddened. "Of course, I'm sorry."

Amalie pulled out the chair next to her. "Would you sit with us for a moment?"

Mary glanced at the kitchen door then at Jakob. She chewed her lip as she contemplated what to do.

Amalie squeezed her hand. Her heart broke for the abused girl. "I promise you will not get in trouble. Henry wouldn't deny the Queen speaking to one of her subjects."

Mary sat down and folded her hands in her lap. She didn't make eye contact with either of them.

Amalie gave Jakob a sad smile. She understood why he felt the need to help the girl. "May I ask, how old are you?"

Mary's eyebrows drew together. Amalie knew the question was odd. "Sixteen."

Amalie nodded. "And is Henry your father?"

Mary shook her head emphatically. "Goodness no. My father was a very sweet man but he passed a couple of years ago. I lost my mother when I was younger so it was just me. Henry took pity on me and let me work here. He gave me a room in the stable."

Jakob leaned forward. "He didn't make you do anything else did he?"

Amalie held her breath, if Mary admitted to being forced into anything sexual, she wouldn't stop Jakob from hurting the man, she'd likely join in.

Mary's eyes widened. "No, he has never done *that* to me."

Amalie and Jakob let out a collective sigh.

Amalie knew her next question might set the girl off but she had to continue on. "Jakob mentioned he thought he saw bruises on you. You don't have to say anything but I want you to know you helped Jakob when he was in need and we want to do the same for you."

Mary's eyes were filled with tears as she looked at Jakob.

When she didn't say anything, Amalie continued on. "When I get back to the castle, I'll likely need to bring in staff that I can trust. How would you feel leaving all of this behind and coming with us? I could use a maid who I know will be loyal to me." Mary's mouth hung wide open. "It won't be terribly taxing, helping me dress, deal with all this hair, and keep my room tidy. All I ask in return is a commitment to me."

Mary sat silent for a full minute. Amalie was starting to worry she was going to say no. The girl dropped to her knees, laid her head on Amalie's lap, and cried. Tears rolled down Amalie's face. She knew what this girl felt. She understood the loneliness, the feelings of despair. She glanced at Jakob and smiled. Did he realize that he and his brothers saved both of them from a life of hopelessness?

Amalie brushed the girl's soft, brown curls from her face. "Sit now, there's a bit more."

Mary brushed the tears from her cheeks as she got back in her chair.

Amalie glanced over at Jakob who was emphatically shaking his head. Amalie pushed forward anyway, after what she witnessed, she had no doubt the girl would handle the news fine. "I know I'm asking for loyalty but there is a specific reason and I want you to go into this fully prepared. It is true when the Gruff brothers found me, I was a large, hairy troll. I started to remember who I was but physically I was still a troll. We found a sorceress who told us love would break the curse and that the four of us together were the key to restoring my place in the Kingdom. Long story short, I kissed Filip and partially shifted. Then I kissed Henrik and shifted to the form you currently see. What I'm trying to explain is that I love them both and I won't choose between them. They are okay with that. When we get to the castle I will not marry, I will live with them. Do you understand?"

Mary's eyes were wide but she nodded. "Who you choose to love is your business. I've heard the stories and can see for myself that you are mostly back to the way you are. I don't need any more proof than that. I'll be honored to serve you and whoever you choose as your life mate." Mary ended her declaration looking at Jakob.

Amalie chuckled. "You're wondering his part in all of this?"

Mary shrugged. "It's not my business."

Amalie glanced at Jakob. His jaw was clenched. "Let's just say his part in all of this is still being determined. For now, you should think of him as my most trusted advisor and protector." She held her hand out to Mary. "So, are you joining us?"

Mary beamed as she shook Amalie's hand. "You had me from the start. I'll be ready in the morning. I'm not sure what to do about Henry though."

Amalie waved her off. "We'll talk to him in the morning. He'll be fine. You pretend everything is normal and let us handle it."

Mary jumped out of her seat as the door to the Inn opened. Henrik and Filip walked in. Filip had a bundle in his hands. They nodded to Mary as she left then collapsed into their chairs. "That was exhausting." Filip set the bag in the center of the table.

Amalie poked at it. "What's this?"

Henrik untied the strings. "It was in the cave with a note from Berit. It's a dress for you and suits for us so we fit in at the castle."

Amalie grabbed the bright pink gown and hugged it close. Her fingers trailed along the sequined bodice. "This may sound vain but I missed ball gowns."

The three brothers laughed at her then inspected the clothes they were given. Henrik whistled. "These are finer than anything we've owned before. How did Berit afford these?"

Jakob shrugged. "I'm sure if you ask her, she'll wink and say *magic*."

Amalie laughed deeply, that's probably exactly what Berit would say. "Besides this unexpected gift, are we all set? Everyone is ready to go?"

Henrik nodded. 'The runners packed up their gear and left immediately. Everyone will be ready by tomorrow night. The closest soldiers will start filtering into the castle in the late afternoon and the rest will follow along as soon as they get there."

Filip agreed. "It will take a couple of hours to get everyone inside but they'll be in place by the time we confront the King and all Hell breaks loose. How did it go here?"

Amalie beamed at Jakob before answering. "Mary has agreed to come with us and will stay in the castle as my maid. As for the people, they are ready to go and will start making their way to the castle once the sun sets." She paused and took a few seconds to look at each man. "All of this is because of you guys. When this is all over the entire Kingdom is going to owe you. I'll have to knight you, everywhere you go people will sing your praises."

She enjoyed watching all three squirm. She loved that they weren't in it for the fortune or the notoriety, they were here for her and she loved each of them for it.

She stood and held her hand out to Henrik. "Will you escort me to bed?"

***

Henrik glanced at his brothers then stood and followed her. Her stomach was in knots as they walked up the steps. She was no longer a virgin but it felt that way as she walked with him. There was a good chance they could be captured or killed tomorrow and she wasn't going to waste any time worrying about it. She had to believe fate knew what she was doing and that they were on the right path. In the meantime, she was going to enjoy every minute she could with her men.

At the top of the stairs, she let him lead the way to their room since she hadn't been there yet. He opened the door for her then quietly stoked the fire. She wondered if he was as nervous as she was.

She waited until he was done before walking over and hugging him. It felt good to stand silently in his arms and just appreciate the moment. She leaned up and grabbed the back of his neck, pulling his face down towards her. Their mouths met; it was better than the first time. This kiss was between two people who knew they were meant to be together.

She pulled back and looked up at him. "I'll give you the choice, we can lay in bed and read until we fall asleep or you can get in that bed and let me pleasure you?"

She saw the fire in his eyes and knew what he wanted. She grabbed his hand and led him to the bed. They took turns undressing each other. As she stood in front of him goosebumps popped up along her skin. He was staring at her, taking in every inch of her body. She knew he didn't see the lumps and distortions that she saw, he didn't care about those things.

His breath had picked up, a faint sheen of sweat broke out across his forehead. He let out a growl as he picked her up, she instinctively wrapped her legs around his waist. She stroked the muscles of his back as he held her. He kneeled on the bed and laid her in the middle, as he came down on top of her, he slid inside in one smooth motion. They didn't need foreplay; she was wet and ready for him the second she saw his naked body.

He kissed her over and over as he thrust inside her, the intimacy of the moment brought tears to her eyes. The rhythm picked up the closer they got to finishing. He reached down and rolled her nipple between his fingers, she moaned as she clamped down on his cock. After a few more strokes she held on as he came.

He laid on top of her, breathing heavily in her ear. He turned and kissed her temple. "I love you, Amalie."

The tears that had threatened earlier poured down her cheeks.

He leaned up to get a better look. "Did I hurt you?"

She shook her head and kissed him. "Quite the opposite, I'm crying because you made me feel so good. I'm just overwhelmed with love."

He kissed her again. "Well get used to it, my brothers and I are going to love you until you're spoiled rotten."

Amalie laughed at the thought. It sounded perfect to her.

Chapter Twenty-Two

Amalie waited by the kitchen door for Henry. He came out wiping his brow. "Your highness, what can I do for you?" Amalie didn't feel bad in the least for what she was about to tell him. "I'm sure you've noticed I don't have a female companion on my journey. I'm sure you can see the issue with this. Mary has agreed to escort me to the castle and stay on in my employ. I realize this leaves you unexpectedly shorthanded and I apologize for that. As soon as I'm secure I'll send a one-time payment for the inconvenience. I'll also include payment for the meals we've eaten and the rooms. Your hospitality won't be forgotten. You are truly one of the heroes of this revolution."

She turned and walked out before he could respond. She hoped the flattery would subdue any anger he might have over losing his serving girl.

Jakob opened the door to the Inn as she was reaching for the handle. "I was coming to check if you were all right?" He glanced over her shoulder at Henry then back to her.

She continued walking. "So far so good, are we

ready to go?"

Jakob led her around the side of the Inn. Filip and Henrik were already on their horses. "Just waiting on you and Mary."

Amalie didn't see the girl anywhere. She pointed at the barn. "Is she in there?"

He nodded.

Amalie walked inside and paused to let her eyes adjust. She saw a head of brown curls peak around a doorframe. Amalie walked toward her. "Are you okay?"

Mary stepped out slowly, glancing in every direction. "Does Henry know yet?"

Amalie should have thought about the girl's fear of the man. "He does and he won't be causing you any issue." She held her hand out to the girl. "Let's go home. You can ride with Jakob; he'll keep you safe."

They walked out of the barn; the three brothers waited patiently. Amalie walked them toward Jakob's horse. "Is it okay if she rides with you?"

Jakob grabbed the girl's small bag. "Of course." He tied the bag to his horse then climbed into the saddle. He reached down and helped Mary sit in front of him.

Amalie winked at him then let Filip help her up on his horse.

He kissed her cheek. "Are you ready for this?"

Amalie leaned back against him and took a deep breath. "No, but I have to be."

Jakob led the party out of the alleyway and

down the street. Amalie discreetly nodded at people as they smiled and gave her thumbs up. She appreciated her supporters not drawing too much attention to them.

She sighed contentedly; she should have realized it was the calm before the storm.

***

The closer they got to the castle the more nauseous Amalie was. She was really doing it, she was really sneaking into the castle and confronting her father. Fear for the three men with her intensified her emotions but she was the princess, she couldn't let it show. "Mary, when it's time for us to sneak in, I'm going to hide you in my old bedroom. I want you out of the way so you aren't hurt or captured. One of us will come get you when it's safe."

Amalie waited until Mary nodded before leading the group to the entrance of a cave.

Jakob paused at the opening. "What is this place?"

Amalie continued walking into the darkness. "It's meant to look like a cave but it's actually an escape route that was built more than one hundred years ago in case the castle was ever under siege. My father and I are the only two living people who know about it."

Amalie prayed the entrance wasn't guarded. It never had been but with her father's heightened paranoia she didn't know what to expect.

Filip reached forward and touched the wall. "I think it's a dead end."

Amalie smiled as she waved him over. "It's a trick, watch." She stepped between a thin crack of the wall and disappeared. She popped her head back out and waved at them to follow. "If anyone does wander in here, they'd find an empty cave and leave."

The group slid behind the fake wall and kept walking. She forgot how long the tunnel was. It felt like an eternity had passed when it was likely only ten minutes. She finally stopped at a wooden door. "This opens up behind another fake wall in one of the underground cellars. We can use the servant's hallways to get up to my room. With the party in full swing, there shouldn't be anyone using them."

She tested the handle, glad to find it wasn't locked.

Jakob grabbed her arm. "Let me go first, just in case."

She stood back and let him take her place. Everyone held their breath as he slowly opened the door. He stepped through and peaked around the fake wall then came back. "It looks empty and it's pretty dark so we should be good."

He waved at Amalie to lead the way. Her hands were sweaty as she crept through the shadows and led them through a few doors. Every noise they heard had her heart jumping into her throat.

Twice they hid in rooms as staff passed by.

By the time they made it to her room, she was shaking with nerves. They slipped inside; Amalie gasped at the sight. Her father had removed everything of hers, there was nothing left except furniture.

Filip walked up and hugged her from behind. "I'm so sorry."

Amalie wanted to cry and rage but she knew that wasn't going to get her anywhere. She straightened her spine, cleared her throat, and turned to the group. "It's nearly midnight, everyone should be well enough into their cups for us to make our way inside. Let's get changed and go."

Mary grabbed the pink gown out of the bag she had been carrying and followed Amalie into a small dressing room off to the side of the bedroom.

Mary blushed as Amalie reached back and untied the dress she was wearing. "This is all new for you, isn't it?"

Mary nodded meekly. "I had no women in my life, I was surprised by your confidence."

Amalie chuckled. "I've had people helping me dress for as long as I can remember. It was second nature; I honestly hadn't even thought about it." She tossed the old dress off to the side. "Help me with this dress then we can just smooth my hair out. I think I'll leave it down since it's one of my defining features." Sadly, if it wasn't for her hair, she didn't think her dad would recognize her. She was still horribly disfigured. She looked down at her cleavage and frowned. "I have really nice breasts you know, you can't see them with this cursed body but they are there and they are gorgeous."

Amalie was glad to see the girl's nervousness melt away as she laughed at Amalie's proclamation.

Once they were done, she stood back and did a circle. "So, how do I look?"

Mary bounced on her toes, "Like a real-life Princess!"

Amalie cracked open the door. "Are you boys decent?"

Three nearly identical yes's echoed around the room. She opened the door wide and strutted out to the middle of the floor. She felt their eyes on her, following every move she made.

She turned and took them in. She had meant to watch them check her out but when she caught sight of them, she lost all thought. They were gorgeous, and all hers. How did she get so lucky? If it took being cursed and thrown in the woods to die for her to find them, she'd do it all over again. "My goodness, you boys clean up nicely. I doubt anyone in the castle is as handsome as you are. I hope there aren't too many pretty young girls here or you may be a distraction." All three shifted nervously, pulling on their sleeves and fixing their hair. They were out of their element and doing it all for her. "Should we go take down the patriarchy?"

Mary stood by the door, Amalie gave her a quick hug. "Lock the door behind us, we'll be back for you soon."

The foursome quietly left and made their way toward the music. All they had to do was follow the music.

A servant passed them in the hall, stopped in his tracks, and stared at her. She wondered what her father had told them. She had been snuck in and out when she was hurt so they likely assumed she died in the carriage accident too. He made the sign of the cross and took off in the opposite direction.

Jakob chuckled at the poor man's fear. "I guess he'll be telling everyone he just saw a ghost. We better hurry before word spreads."

The doors to the ballroom were wide open. Amalie shook out her nerves then stepped into view. She took strength from the three men encircling her. As people caught sight of them, they stopped talking and gawked. Amalie made her way to the front of the room, the King was on a dais with four women fawning over him. The musicians picked up on the tone of the room and stopped playing.

Amalie stopped at the edge of the platform. "Father."

The King froze. He stared at her, first shocked, then angry. "Guards, get these imposters out of here."

They were quickly surrounded. Amalie didn't back down. "You don't recognize your own daughter?"

He stood up, his face purple as he shouted. "My

daughter is dead. I don't know who or what you are but you are not my Amalie."

For a brief second Amalie believed him. Did he really think she was an imposter? She turned and scanned the crowd. She recognized many of the aristocracies. "I am Princess Amalie and I'm here to accuse my father of treason. He murdered your Queen and when I managed to survive, he had me cursed into a troll and thrown away like a wild animal."

The room exploded as everyone began speaking at once. She could hear people questioning her looks, the word hideous was said more than once.

The King's roar echoed around the room. "Silence!"

Amalie turned back to look at her father who had walked closer. He paused and turned his head to the side, listening to something. "What is that sound."

Amalie grinned. "The sound of your demise."

Chapter Twenty-Three

A malie walked up on the stage and faced the crowd again. "The Kingdom has had enough. Your people, the ones who depend on you for survival are outside demanding retribution." She turned and faced her father. "I spent weeks traveling through the villages, they saw firsthand as the curse started to slowly break and I began the shift back to myself. Admit what you've done and I'll go easy on you."

Soldiers ran in from the hall. "Sire, there's a mob outside, they were trying to breach the walls and someone opened the gate and let them in. You need to get to safety."

He turned his rage at Amalie. "Why couldn't you just stay dead?" He turned to the guards still surrounding the stage. "I gave you an order to arrest them, now do it."

All at once, hell broke loose. As the guards reached for the brothers they fought back. More guards ran into the hall and shocked the crowd as they turned on the other guards and helped the brothers fight them off.

Amalie turned to her father and sighed. "You're

going to lose, give up now." She didn't see the knife in his hand, she was too busy staring at the evil smirk on his face. His dagger plunged into her stomach.

Jakob roared as he grabbed a sword from the nearest guard and jumped on the stage. He plunged it straight into the King's heart then fell to his knees next to Amalie.

As she lay on the ground, gasping in pain, tears rolled down her cheeks. It wasn't fair that her father was going to win after all.

Jakob wrapped his arms around her and held her against his chest. Filip and Henrik were next to her. It was fitting that they would be together as she took her last breath.

Jakob sobbed against her head. "I'm sorry we weren't strong enough to protect you. I tried so hard not to love you but I couldn't stop it. You're a part of me and I was stupid not to follow my heart."

She gasped for air one last time before taking her last breath. "Wait, no." He lifted her chin and kissed her. A final tear rolled down her cheek, she could die happy knowing Jakob did love her.

Chapter Twenty-Four

Jakob stood staring out the window of the castle. It had been three days since his life was forever altered as he kissed his dying Princess.

Henrik and Filip walked up and stood on either side of him. Henrik rested a hand on his shoulder. "How are you holding up?"

Jakob stared out the window, still struggling to look his brothers in the face. "I haven't forgiven myself yet if that's what you're asking."

Filip turned and leaned against the window. "You're being too hard on yourself. What Amalie had offered was a lot to ask any man to accept. She didn't blame you for taking so long to accept her, and neither did we."

Jakob quirked an eyebrow at him. "And now? If I had kissed her sooner, she could have been fully shifted before the confrontation. The crowd would have been on her side immediately. Instead, she died knowing everyone in the room called her hideous and disgusting."

Henrik grabbed his brother and shook him. "Enough of this. The pity party is over. It's time for you to go."

Jakob knew his brothers were right, it was time to move on and accept the part he had played. He walked to the door and took one last deep breath before walking through it.

The sight before him took his breath away. Amalie stood in front of the fire, the light outlining her curves through the sheer nightgown she wore.

She turned and smiled. "It's about time you came to see me. You are stubborn, aren't you?"

He walked over and scooped her up. He nuzzled her neck as he walked to the bed. "I'm sorry, I still feel like an ass."

She rolled her eyes at him. "It all worked out in the end. Your kiss broke the curse."

He gently laid her on the bed. "If it weren't for Berit storming the castle with the mob you wouldn't be alive right now."

Amalie pulled her nightgown off then reached for him. "That's why I'm not upset. Everything happened exactly how fate wanted it to. She was meant to be there at that moment and save my life."

He knew she was right. Although the hour they sat outside her bedroom door while Berit worked on her was excruciating and he would have preferred fate had spared them that experience.

She watched him as he stripped, her breathing sped up as he climbed on top of her. She pulled his head close. "Now enough of this, I've wanted you for weeks. Show me what I've been missing out on."

Jakob growled as the overwhelming need to claim her engulfed him. He wanted to be inside her, making her moan, making her his. His lips brushed against her skin, he teased her with kisses on her neck, her breasts, down to her stomach. He flicked his tongue across her nipple.

Her fingers curled in his hair. "Jesus, you're torturing me."

He pressed his palm against her clit but didn't move it. "Are you in a hurry?"

She thrust her hips repeatedly, trying to force his hand to move. "Well, kind of," she panted, "we can take it slow next time. Right now, I just want to fuck you."

He glanced down at her stomach where there should have been a wound. "You're sure we can do this?"

She let out a deep breath then shoved him to his back and climbed on top. "Berit used her magic, it's as if it never happened." She leaned up on her knees, the tip of his cock at her opening. "Now, as your Queen, I demand you lay there and let me do what I want with your body."

His throat went dry. "I'll do as you command."

They moaned in unison as she slid down on top of his cock. Neither moved for a few seconds, the feeling of being buried deep was too good to not savor.

He grabbed her hips and let her control the rhythm, her breasts bounced as she rode him hard. She was glorious to watch. He reached down and rubbed her clit with his thumb. She tightened around him, her head thrown back. Jakob wanted more. "I want you to look at me while you come. Keep your eyes open, let me watch you."

She looked down at him and smiled. "I'll do as you command."

He reached up with his other hand and squeezed her nipple. She gasped and picked up the pace. His heart was racing, he couldn't last much longer. He saw the moment she came, it was beautiful and just enough to push him over the edge. He shouted as he came, she squeezed him, milking him for every drop he had.

She collapsed on top of him, panting heavily. Jakob wrapped his arms around her and held on tight. His breath was stolen from him, not from exertion though, from the idea that he almost missed out on a life with her. How did he ever think he could deny she was his Queen, his mate, the woman he would die for.

Epilogue

The entire kingdom had come to the palace to celebrate the crowning of their Queen. They waited outside, watching the balcony for her to be presented, chanting her name.

Amalie felt the weight of the crown on her head both literally and figuratively. It was done, she was now the ruler of her people.

Jakob, Henrik, and Filip stood at the balcony doors waiting for her. She still couldn't believe this was her life now. She had a maid that was quickly becoming a best friend, three men who adored her, and their parents who accepted her as a daughter without question.

Henrik and Filip had gone to get them a few days earlier. They were moved into the palace, tended to by the castle healer, and even given some tea by Berit. They had started showing an improvement almost immediately. Amalie still suspected there was something strange about the tea.

She kissed the boy's parents on their cheeks and walked towards her future, her lovers, and her kingdom.

The End

ABOUT THE AUTHOR

Cassidy lives in the Tampa, Florida area with her high school sweetheart, their three children, her dog Flynn who she loves obsessively, and her grand dog. She loves reading and going to the movies. She also loves to travel and hopes to one day watch a baseball game in every MLB stadium in the country.

To learn more about Cassidy please visit her online at www.cassidykoconnor.com.

You can also find her on Facebook at www.facebook.com/cassidykoconnorauthor

She always welcomes new friends and encourages readers to reach out to her.

Other Books by the Author